# FIGHT
# FOREVER

—PEAK VALLEY FOREVER SERIES—

## AMANDA LEE DIXON

Fight Forever

Amanda Lee Dixon

# Table of Contents

Fight Forever

# *Prologue*

"You want to live here? In this ramshackle house?" Luke eyes me curiously. We are laid out on a blanket in his backyard staring up at the stars. An early summer heatwave hit, turning the house into a stuffy hot box, driving us outside where the cicadas are buzzing and the stars are twinkling.

"I love this house. It may not be pretty now, but it has potential," I say, curling closer into his side, placing my chin on his chest so I can look into Luke's warm blue eyes. I love his eyes, full of mischief and a softness whenever I catch him watching me.

"I rather build you a house, Amber," Luke says, giving me a small squeeze. "Your dream home."

"I like this house. It feels... I don't know, like it's meant to be our place." I shrug, rolling off Luke and lay on my back. I stare at the house Luke grew up in—the home I see us starting our lives in, where we will raise our children, and grow old together.

It's a two-story house with white paint that is covered in dirt from years of neglect. The peeling paint is so dingy, the house is really more of a gray color, but I can picture it a gleaming white with a red door and crystal-clear picture windows. I see past the splintering wooden porch, rotten window frames, and missing shutters. I see what the house could be, not what it is.

The interior is just as bad as the exterior, with scuffed wooden floors, grimy walls that haven't been cleaned in years, missing cabinet doors, and dated appliances, but there is beauty hiding underneath. The open-concept floorplan, with its large kitchen, could comfortably accommodate a growing family. I see us having Sunday dinners with all of Luke's brothers and my own family sitting around his mother's long dining room table.

So what if all the doors squeak? They can be oiled. Who cares if the bathrooms look straight out of the '70s? Luke and I can update them together, turn them into mini-spa retreats. The possibilities are endless.

Luke shifts to his side, propping himself on an elbow as his eyes focus on my mouth. "This place has some rotten memories."

"But you had some good memories, too," I say, turning my head to face him. He's thinking about his dad, who is passed out in his recliner, oblivious to the world around him and the pain he causes his sons. "Before your mom died."

Sadness clouds Luke's beautiful blue eyes whenever his mom is mentioned. She died too young, leaving behind four sons who cherished her and a husband who lost himself to alcohol, drinking his pain away.

Despite the crappy hand Luke was dealt, he managed to stay kind and charming. Shouldering the burden to care for his younger brothers and stepping into shoes meant for an adult. I admire him more every day when I see him step up, yet not sacrificing his dreams.

"Do you know how much I love you?" Luke asks and his blue eyes darken as he searches mine with desperation, as if he's afraid I'll disappear.

I don't answer him with words but with a kiss that conveys more than words could ever say.

A kiss that binds us together, that quickens my pulse and takes my breath away.

Our love is all-consuming, so deep it merges our souls. He's it for me. My one and only love.

Until he wasn't…

Until he broke all his promises.

Until he broke my heart.

Broke me.

# 1

## - Luke -

*Fifteen years later*

"We are gathered here today to join this man and this woman in holy matrimony," Peak Valley's Community Church minister speaks out to the guests. There are hundreds of people here to witness the wedding that will go down in Peak Valley history. Even I can't believe it's happening. "If anyone has any objections, please speak now or forever hold your peace."

"I better not hear anyone one of you object!" Burns snaps to the guests, glaring at them. He never was a man of subtlety.

Burns has been the closest thing I have had to a father. Mine checked out not long after my mother died in a car accident when I was barely a teenager. He forgot he had four sons unless we got in his way, then hell broke loose. He was mean and drank his sorrows away until he died. I can't imagine what we would have become if it wasn't for Burns. I'm honored he asked me and my brothers to stand with him to tie the knot.

"Then do you, Alvin Burns, take Janet Johnson to be your lawfully wedded wife?" the preacher asks, pulling Burns' attention back to his blushing bride.

"Hell yeah, I do!" he whoops, a toothy grin stretches across his wrinkled face, and he looks years younger than a man in his eighties.

"Do you, Janet Johnson, take Alvin Burns to be your lawfully wedded husband?"

"I do," Miss Janet politely says with a big smile and a twinkle in her eye.

"Can I kiss my woman now?" Burns asks the minister eagerly with raised eyebrows. The pride that shines in his eyes spreads a wide smile across my face. Call me a sucker for weddings but seeing a man gaze at his woman as if she is the only person in the room pulls at my heartstrings.

Another emotion, envy maybe, but it doesn't really describe the longing I have to be in Burns' shoes, with one person in particular, but she isn't giving me the time of day.

"You may kiss the bride." The minister nods with a chuckle, reminding me I have best man duties I should be focusing on. Burns wastes no time planting what I can only describe as an old man kiss on Miss Janet… wait now, Mrs. Burns.

Guests erupt into cheers and several aren't afraid to grumble as they stand for the happy couple, who continue to kiss. Let's be honest, they are full-on making out, and it isn't a sight I want permanently fixed in my brain. Looking away, my eyes zero in on their target. The woman who haunts my waking and sleeping hours, Amber.

She's stunning in a red '50s-inspired bridesmaid dress. The sweetheart neckline draws my eyes to her cleavage before the dress flares out just above her knees. I silently beg her to look at me, just one glance this way. I sound desperate, but I have been in love with this woman for over fifteen years. I knew she was it for me after our first date, but I blew it not long after that. No, I didn't blow it… I destroyed it.

"You're drooling," Jax, my youngest brother, says from the end of the groomsmen line.

I face my annoying baby brother and my other equally annoying brother, Eric, who both watch me with smug smiles. I mentally note to leave their asses here when I head for the reception. "Just ask her out already."

"He can't." Eric chuckles. "She won't give him the time of day."

"Rough," Jax says. "Now move."

The new Mr. and Mrs. Burns step away from the altar and head down the aisle. I step from the altar as Amber steps down, sticking out my elbow. She takes it, and warmth spreads over me like melted butter. I could be putty in her hand if she would only pay me a little attention.

Her smile is dazzling, showing off her white teeth. The whole church receives her smile, except for me. Her hand, the slight pressure it makes, is precious—and I know it's all I will get from her. She is walking with me out of respect and love for Burns and Miss Janet… I mean, the new Mrs. Burns. I reach across and place my hand over hers, wishing she knew just how sorry I am with that one touch. Two emerald eyes flare up at me with annoyance, and I know I shouldn't smile, but I love when she gets fired up.

The slow march down the aisle ends all too soon as we file out of the church and line up to greet everyone who has come to witness the cranky bastard Burns get married. Half the town is here because of the bet—which I started and feel no shame about it. All of us expected Miss Janet to kill him before making it down the aisle. Love truly is blind, I guess.

Amber releases my elbow the moment we line up, continuing to ignore me as guests shuffle past, shaking our hands. She's shivering from the cool autumn air, so I remove my jacket and wrap it around her shoulders. Before she can protest, someone comes up to shake her hand, telling her how beautiful she is before they glance at me and then back at her with a knowing smile. Her glowing green eyes ignite with anger as they start to coo at how cute we look together. We *are* an attractive couple. Our babies would have been beautiful. She mutters a curse under her breath as another pudgy woman clutches her hands to her chest and sighs when she steps up to us.

"You two are so adorable. I'm glad you found your way back to each other," she says. Thank goodness we're in a church, or that sharp tongue of Amber's would get her in trouble.

"How long do we have to stand here?" Burns stage-whispers to Mrs. Burns. *Ha! Got it right this time.*

"Until everyone has been thanked for coming." Mrs. Burns pats his shoulder with a sweet smile. The woman was blessed with the patience of a saint. She's got to be a saint for putting up with Burns—or maybe she's a pod person.

"Settle down, Alvin, or you're likely to anger the missus before you get to the wedding night festivities," Jax says at the end of the line, not giving a hoot that we stand in a house of worship. The boy did grow up half-wild at no fault of his own.

"You boys ever call me Alvin, and I'll tan your hide," Burns threatens. "Oh, pastor . . .. Thank you for getting us hitched."

"My pleasure," the pastor says as he moves to shake the happy couple's hands. "And I'll be seeing you this Sunday for service."

"Of course, you will." Mrs. Burns speaks for them as Burns tries to hide his grimace. Biting my tongue to smoother my laugh, I quickly shake the pastor's hand, who shuffles past us Colson boys. I don't blame him—we weren't exactly upstanding teenagers and pulled our share of pranks on the poor pastor. Nothing too terrible, but I do think we may have gone a bit too far when we tried to convince him that the church was haunted.

"Let's get moving, we have a party to start." Burns turns to us, waving his hands toward the door.

"Dawn, do you have room for me to ride over to Benny's?" Amber asks my soon-to-be sister-in-law.

"You can ride with me," I cut in, sending Dawn a very pointed stare. She can read my brother Clint's mind, so she should be able to read mine and make up an excuse that works in my favor.

"I didn't ask you," Amber says, rolling her eyes and crossing her arms underneath my jacket she has yet to take off. I'm calling that a win. A pitiful win, but a win, nonetheless. Or am I overthinking things?

"Yes, you can ride with us," Dawn says, hiding her smile rather poorly and utterly letting me down. *Some soon-to-be sister-in-law she is.*

"I should probably drive you lovely ladies," I attempt again, because like I said, I have no shame and Amber ignoring me, blowing me off, and overall standoffishness is getting under my skin. "Clint's still in a sling and has no business driving."

"I was cleared to drive last week," Clint, a man of few words, says with a smirk. His left arm is still in a sling from the two bullets he took to the shoulder only a few weeks ago. His right arm pulls his new fiancée close to his side, and envy gut-punches me again.

"Can we roll?" Jax interrupts, giving me a cheesy wink as his hands clamp around my shoulders and shakes me a little. "I'm ready for a drink."

"We don't have time to argue, and I need to get to my kids," Amber says. She takes my jacket off and thrusts it toward me. "I'm riding with Clint and Dawn."

"Keep it," I say and turn away from her. *Damn.*

"You just don't know when to give up," Jax jokes when we are out of hearing distance from Amber.

"Shut it, Jax," I say, punching him in the shoulder.

"He has a point," Eric pipes in, slapping me on the back. "Why are you trying so hard?"

"I'll tell you when you tell me what's going on between you and Sarah?" I return, eyeing him with a smug grin. Sarah is Amber's sister and like Amber, was also a bridesmaid in Burns' wedding.

18

Since her arrival in town a few weeks ago to help Dawn and Clint clean up some drama that left two bullet holes in my brother and Eric and Sarah beat up from a car wreck, the two have been inseparable.

"Eric and Sarah are just as disastrous as you and Amber," Jax says before ducking his head and climbing into the backseat of my pick-up truck.

"Shut it, Jax."

"Now I know why I haven't been home in ten years. All you guys ever say to me is 'Shut it, Jax'."

"Say something worth listening to and we won't have to tell you to shut it." Eric smiles over his shoulder at Jax.

"Why are you and Sarah so disastrous?" This is the first I knew the two were ever a thing. When I left for the military, Eric was banging any available girl who gave him the time of day.

Eric doesn't say anything at first, but finally sighs and says, "We were a thing for a minute, but it didn't work out . . .."

"It wasn't a minute; it was two years. And if I recall, you ended it when she left for college," Jax shares. "You broke her heart the same way Luke broke Amber's. You both are lucky the

Baker women are even talking to you. Hell, I don't even know why Benny lets you both frequent his establishment."

Amber's dad owns *Benny's Bar*, the only decent place to get a cold beer in Peak Valley. It also happened to be my only connection to Amber. She was the night bartender before Dawn took over for her. Now she's an ER nurse working the night shift.

"Shut it, Jax," Eric says again, his annoyance with the situation etched across his face.

He raises his hands up in surrender. "Only speaking the truth."

"At least Amber's pissed. That means I have a shot," I say as I pull out of the church parking lot onto Peak Valley's main road.

"Where did you come up with that kind of logic?" Eric asks.

"If she's pissed, it means she still cares. I'd be worried if she was civil," I say with a knowing smile and a wink.

"You think because she doesn't want to have anything to do with you, she's still in love with you?" Eric asks with narrowed eyes.

"It makes sense." Jax shrugs. "Kind of like playing hard to get."

"It doesn't make any sense," Eric sputters, looking more agitated and glaring back at Jax. "Amber is an adult; I don't think she's playing any head games. I think she's still bitter about your epic screw up."

"It wasn't *my* screw up," I growl, tightening my hands on the steering wheel.

"Whatever. It was your stupidity that caused you two to break up. It doesn't matter if you were at fault or not." Eric sighs. "I still think you're wasting your time trying to get back with her."

"I would agree if I didn't think she cared, but she does . . .. She just doesn't want to admit it." I flash my signature smile while pulling into *Clint's Autobody Shop* parking lot that sits across the street from a packed *Benny's Bar*.

"I hope Dawn and Miss Janet made enough food . . . it looks like the whole town is here," Jax says as we climb out of my truck and cross the street toward *Benny's*.

"Mrs. Burns," I correct with a wink. "It's surreal the old man is married and to such a lovely woman."

The reception is in full swing when we walk through the entrance. A line has formed around the buffet and most of the tables are packed with people. For a bar that mostly smells like beer and burgers, the transformation into a wedding reception is strange. Sheer red and cream fabric drape from the ceiling and around the walls, hiding the wood paneling and dingy ceiling. The tables and chairs are covered in cream-colored fabric with red ribbons, and small candles surrounding roses in short vases center the tables.

"Wow, this place looks almost fancy," Jax says as he looks around the place. I have to admit that the ladies did a wonderful job on the place. "I'm starving, let's get in line."

"Do they expect us to sit at the main table?" Eric asks as we shuffle our way toward the buffet line.

"That was my idea," I say, looking over at the main table that was reserved for the wedding party. "Easiest way to get Amber to sit next to me."

"You're hopeless," Eric groans.

# 2

## - Amber -

"Please welcome the new Mr. and Mrs. Alvin Burns!" the DJ says over the mic as Burns and Janet walk into the reception, their smiles wide across their wrinkled faces. Seeing the two gaze into each other's eyes as they walk in with so much love should make me want to cry out of love and joy for them, but all I feel is envy. Lots and lots of envy.

"Kiss, kiss, kiss," the crowd cries out to the happy couple. I force myself to chime in as they make their way to the main table. I really am happy for them—they deserve happiness—but something about weddings brings out my ugly side.

Who am I kidding? I really don't like weddings. They're supposed to be a promise of love but in my experience, promises of love are just words and mean nothing.

Burns pulls Janet in close and smacks his lips against hers in what can only be described as cute yet off-putting. Everyone cheers as their kiss grows more intimate. The cheers fade as the happy couple's innocent kiss turns into an obscene make-out session.

"Is it wrong to call that gross when it's their wedding day?" Luke leans in from his seat next to me. His woodsy scent invades my nostrils. He still smells like he did fifteen years ago, and I hate that I love that scent.

"I think they are sweet," I lie but can't hide the grimace on my face when Burns grabs Janet's backside. "Okay, that's gross."

"Have I told you how beautiful you look?" Luke says, smiling down at me. His blue eyes shine with mischief that takes me back to when we were younger, back when life wasn't so complicated.

"Yes, multiple times," I say trying not to swoon. Every time he told me I was beautiful, a swarm of butterflies swirled around in my stomach. I wish my head and body would get on the same page because no matter how charming Luke is to me, I am never giving him a second chance.

Yeah, yeah, I know never say never, but when it comes to Luke, I mean never.

"I like how you did your hair." His eyes scan over my hair like a caress that causes me to shiver. "The loopy things are nice."

"Loopy things?"

"Yeah, the loops in your hair." His eyes find mine, and that charming smile of his falters when I narrow my eyes at him.

"It's styled to match the dress." Crossing my arms, I try to convey my annoyance, hoping Luke doesn't have the ability to read my real thoughts like he once was able to do. "Are we really doing this?"

"Doing what?"

"Having pleasant small talk?"

"Well, I would like to do more than just pleasant small talk . . .." He smirks down at me and leans in a little closer. My pulse quickens as my body tingles with familiar awareness of Luke. No matter how hard I try to hate him, the longing for him won't fade. There has to be a pill or hypnosis or something that could make it go away.

Looking into those familiar eyes, I can't help but notice the changes from the young man I fell in love with and the man standing before me. He's taller, stronger, with a hard edge to him that comes from being in the military for the last fifteen years. His sleek black hair is shorter, and with several days' worth of facial hair, he has a rugged attractiveness to him that is opposite of the boy I remember.

When Luke left fifteen years ago, his charm and his blue eyes, which were so full of laughter, dulled. It broke my heart to see him transform right before my eyes, but looking at him now, they are brighter, filled with mischief and something I can't quite describe. It scares me how much I missed them, but never has to mean never. Has to.

"Can I get you a drink?" He breaks into my thoughts, still aiming that full, mega-watt smile at me.

The cocky jerk knows exactly what he's doing to me. "No, I'm fine," I snap with a scowl.

The feel of his hand on my lower back sends a wave of heat to my core, and I mentally yell at myself for allowing such an innocent touch trigger such a fierce reaction. Before I can jerk away, he steps back, and a full-body flush heats my skin.

"I think that is the most civil I have seen the two of you," Dawn says from her seat next to me with a knowing smile.

"I must be losing my touch," I say with a shrug. "I'm going to find my kids and hope my parents are not spoiling them into rotten little beasts."

"Hurry back. Clint is pouting," Dawn says. Her smile radiates with love as she looks over at her fiancé.

"I'm not pouting," he grunts with narrowed eyes. "I just don't see why I have to still wear this suit."

"Get used to it, you'll be wearing it again soon enough at your own wedding," I say with a chuckle. I rise from my chair and scan the room. Internally I sigh, another wedding. And if Eric and Sarah are reuniting their lost love, there is sure to be a third wedding.

A few tables away, my parents are enjoying their food with my son Matt, though Emily doesn't appear to be anywhere. A flicker of worry quickens my step as I weave through the crowded bar-turned-reception hall. "Where's Emily?"

"Hey, Amber," my mom greets me with her warm smile. Her mousy brown hair curls around her heart-shaped face that shines with pride. "She went to get a cupcake."

"Alone?"

"Relax, you can see her from here." She points toward the buffet table where Emily is unsuccessfully reaching across the table for the cupcake stand.

Even on her tiptoes, Emily is inches away from the cupcakes. I start to head toward her when Luke steps up, plucking a cupcake off the stand and offers it to her. Such a simple act, but it scrapes at the walls around my heart, demanding I take notice how Emily lights up with delight, snatching the cupcake before she tilts her head all the way back to look up at the man who came to her aid.

Luke gets down on one knee, though he still towers over her as he speaks to her. She hops from one foot to the other, and I can hear her cheerful laughter from where I stand.

This is the first time Luke has been near my kids, and seeing him interact with Emily, making her laugh, hurts in a way I never expected. A painful, longing kind of hurt.

"Mom, can I go sit with Clint?" my son Matt asks, and I'm thankful for the distraction.

"Yes, but don't pester him too much. He's still healing." I try to sound normal, but I know my voice comes out sounding breathy and shaken.

"Emily seems to have made a new friend," Mom says with a teasing smile.

"Don't start, Mom." I inhale deeply, wishing I accepted Luke's offer for a drink.

"Mommy!" Emily's excited little voice calls out as she rushes toward me. "Mommy, willyoudancewithluke?"

"Slow down, sweetie." I scoop up my baby girl and sit her on my lap. "Now, what did you say?"

"Will you dance with Luke? He's my new friend." Her toothless smile is smeared with icing. "Did you know he's a giant?" she stage-whispers with wide eyes.

Glancing up, I find Luke watching me with those warm blue eyes and that charming, cocky grin I want to loathe. Tipping his beer bottle in salute toward me, he winks as Emily bounces energetically in my lap.

"Will you dance with Luke?" she asks again. Her sticky hands reach up and pull my face, turning it to look at her. "He's my friend."

*That arrogant, cocky bastard!*

"Yeah, Amber, will you dance with Luke?" Mom says, failing to hide her laughter. She always was Team Luke—even when he broke my heart. She held onto hope that we would get back together.

Looking at my dad, he raises his hands and says, "Don't look at me. You're capable of saying no."

"Emily, I don't want to dance." I look into her emerald eyes that are identical to mine. The jubilance fades, along with her smile, and I feel like the worst mom in the world.

"B-but he wants to dance with you," she says with her signature pout. "Please, Mom, he really, *really* wants to dance with you. He told me so."

"Son of a motherless goat," I groan and pull Emily into a hug. Standing, I walk her over to my dad and put her in his lap. "One dance, but no more. And you two," I point to my parents, "are supposed to be on *my* side."

Mom smiles innocently. "Honey, we are on your side; you're just too stubborn to see what's good for you."

Emily shoots Luke a thumbs up while trying to wink, but it looks more like spastic blinking. Turning away from my traitorous family, I glare at Luke, who looks very happy for a man who is about to meet his maker.

"Using my kid? Really, Luke? That's low, even for you."

Luke takes a step into my personal space and his hand wraps around my hip. The touch, like all his other touches, sets my heart racing and my body hums with familiar awareness.

"When it comes to you, I'm a man with no shame," he says with a smirk, his fingers on my hip squeezing slightly.

"Let's get this over with," I say with as much haughtiness I can summon. I pull from his grip, ignoring the twinge of guilt for being scornful, but with Luke, its my only defense.

Luke's velvety laugh follows me as I lead us to the dance floor, but I'm too uneasy for it to affect me. Before I even make it to the dance floor, his hand hits my lower back and my insides melt.

He's too close, way too close. Hesitating, he presses me forward onto the dance floor. Turning too fast, I nearly lose my balance before he steadies me, pulling me flush against his chest. I can hear the chuckle in his voice. "Steady there, darlin'." That devasting smile used to make me feel safe, but now I feel anything but safe.

I blank my face of all emotion as I clear my throat. "One dance."

"The song's half over, you'll have to put up with me through the next song or poor Emily might insist on another dance," he says, leaning in close to my ear, his breath warm against my neck. How I want to loathe this man. "Do you remember the last time we danced together?"

"How could I forget? You coerced me at this year's Fall Festival." I roll my eyes while he grabs my arm and puts it on his shoulder. My other arm follows on its own—that all too familiar feeling floods my system. My body sings as if it knows it's meant to be in his arms, and it takes all my effort not to rest my head on his chest.

"Darla had me in her sights, it would have been a blood bath if she got her claws in me," he says with a laughing smile, his warm blue eyes twinkle as he sways us around the dance floor.

"I wish she did," I mutter and look away from him.

His chuckle vibrates against my chest. "You plan to hate me for the rest of our lives?" He swings me out, snatching my hand and clumsily twirling me before pulling me back in.

"I don't hate you . . ." I say a little breathless from the sudden twirl and look up at him between narrowed eyes. "I dislike you, but I don't hate you."

He raises a brow. "Could've fooled me."

"Luke—"

"It's been fifteen years, Amber. How long do you plan to punish me?" he asks softly, stopping us from dancing. His penetrating stare searches for understanding, but how do I tell him I have to punish him, I have to hold him at arm's length because I had him once and he broke me. I lost myself after he left, and it took years to find myself again. I can't risk being broken again. I won't survive it.

"I should get back to Emily," I say as I pull from his grip. His eyes shine with an emotion I don't want to begin to analyze and I turn my back on the man who may still own my soul.

# Fight Forever

# 3

# - Luke -

"Did you guys know Benny plans to sell his bar?" Jax asks, coming from the bar where he was chatting with Benny.

"Sarah mentioned he was thinking about it," Eric says to my right.

"He said he was holding off selling because of Amber and then Dawn came along, but now that she's leaving…"

I look over at Clint with surprise. "Dawn's leaving?"

"She's going to help at the shop doing the bookwork. I don't want her on her feet all the time now that she's expecting." Clint shrugs, his face devoid of emotion, the scar our father gave him puckering his mouth into a permanent scowl.

"I think it's time I look into a new investment." Jax smiles over his beer bottle before taking a long drink.

"What the hell does that mean?" Eric frowns at our youngest brother. "Why do you always speak in riddles?"

"It means, I'm thinking about giving Benny an offer," he says with a roguish smile.

"You want to move back to Peak Valley? I thought you preferred the nomadic lifestyle?" I say, looking around for a certain brunette who has been avoiding me since our spat on the dance floor.

"I've been thinking about laying down some roots lately . . . just haven't found the right opportunity."

"All four Colson boys back in Peak Valley," Sheriff Warren McKnight says from behind us. We all turn to face the dipshit who caused us trouble back in the day.

Since moving back home, he's managed to pull me over twice for some bullshit reason. The town's golden boy all grown up with a badge giving him too much of a God complex. If only the residents of Peak Valley knew his true colors.

"Got something to say, McKnight?" Eric scratches his jaw, sizing the sheriff up. All of us Colson boys have had beef with McKnight Senior, but Eric and McKnight were bitter enemies.

"Just doing my civic duty. You boys stay out of trouble now." He smirks before making his way to Sarah. He glances over his shoulder and winks.

"Bastard," Eric mutters under his breath before chugging his beer. "I need another beer, anyone else need one?"

"I'm good," I say, glancing yet again at Amber, who's sitting with her parents and Dawn. Emily is sitting in her lap playing with her hair and the sight fills me with a yearning that hasn't gone away these past fifteen years.

"You sure?" Eric asks with an arched brow. "Rejection is cured with a stiff drink."

"Fuck off." I shove him and he heads for the bar where Sarah is chatting with Sheriff McKnight.

"Dawn mentioned the insurance company was giving Amber the runaround," Clint says in that quiet manner of his.

"Why are you telling me this?" I ask, searching Clint's face. He isn't much for talking and when he tells you something, its usually for a reason.

"So you don't piss her off more than you normally do. She's got enough on her plate." He claps my shoulder with his good hand.

A few months ago, a fire at Dawn's house spread, consuming Amber's house next door. She lost everything. Fortunately, no one was hurt, but I know she had to move her and the kids to her parents' small home while she slowly pieced her life back together.

"Why so protective, Clint?" I snap, feeling a little territorial.

"She and Dawn are tight. You piss Amber off, you piss Dawn off... and then I have to deal with them both," Clint says with narrowed eyes. "Don't you think it's time to move on?"

"No," I say dryly. Moving on isn't an option. Moving on is giving up, and I already did that once. I won't do it again.

# 4

# - Amber -

"Matt, that was a great game!" I exclaim as a tired Matt walks over to me after his basketball game. The gymnasium is filled with parents and kids scrambling for seats or trying to shuffle out of the way for the next game. "You guys slaughtered the other team." I pull him in for a sweaty hug. Oh, sweet mother of pearl, he smells. We definitely need to have a chat about deodorant.

"Yeah, they weren't that tough. I like it better when the games are tough," he says, returning the hug with a quick pat.

A throat clears behind me and I turn to see the man I use to call my husband standing next to his new wife. They never sit in the team section where the other parents sit. They are usually somewhere out of sight, which is fine by me.

Both look out of place in the middle of the gymnasium—Henry in a suit that drips 'I have tons of money' and DeeDee looks like she walked right out of a fashion magazine.

"Henry, I'm glad you made the game." I give him a forced smile.

"Of course, I made the game," he says with a frown. I bite my tongue so I don't remind him that he missed last weekend's game due to some client meeting he had to attend. The man sells insurance to the wealthy—something that was made easier for him when he met DeeDee, a socialite in Kansas City. Her connections set him up with more success in the insurance business than he had when we were married.

"Matt, I'm disappointed. You had four points less than your last game. Do you want your average to go down?"

"Henry—"

He holds his hand up to cut me off. "I'm talking to my son." He turns his frown back to Matt. "I'm paying a lot of money so you can play in a competitive league. I'm driving two hours out of my way to be here to watch you play and two hours back. That is a lot of time wasted, and I don't want to waste it watching you sit on the bench. I expect to see better stats. And why *did* you sit on the bench for half of the last quarter?"

"We were up by fifteen points; the coach wanted the second-string players to get some more play time," Matt answers while looking down at his feet. The bright smile he was wearing is gone.

"I think I'll have a little chat with your coach," Henry sniffs, looking from a defeated Matt to me. "Can I have a word?"

"Matt, run over to Papa," I say softly to Matt, patting his shoulder, wishing I could tell Henry off. I help pay Matt's league fees and they are steep, but it is a good league. Matt has shown promise, but he's still young; who knows if basketball will be something he is into when he hits high school or even college? I want him to have fun, not spend his entire childhood preparing for adulthood.

Looking at Henry with barely contained anger, I don't even recognize the man who stands before me. He isn't the same man I married eleven years ago. The man I married was the first man to make me laugh after Luke broke me. He was caring, ambitious, and fun; now he's just ambitious and cold. They say money will do that to you, but I don't think it is the money that turned him cold— I think it is the want for more money and more prestige that has corrupted him.

"How is the home situation?" Henry asks, getting to the point before Matt is out of earshot. Matt glances over his shoulder and I smile at him, hoping he doesn't worry. I have noticed his shoulders droop more lately. He's carrying a weight on his shoulders he shouldn't have to carry, but he won't talk to me, either.

"What do you mean, Henry?" I ask, trying not to sound edgy as I look away from my son and into Henry's calculating eyes.

"Are you still living with your parents?"

"Yes," I hiss, shoving my hands into my pockets so I won't be tempted to slap him.

"I could look into the insurance problems if you want…" He flashes a small smile I'm familiar with. He's laughing at me and honestly, I can't blame him. I used to be married to a man who sells insurance. You'd think I would know a good home insurance policy—particularly one that covers fire.

"No, thank you. Sarah is looking into it for me," I say with a tight smile.

"So, you plan to stay with your parents indefinitely?"

"The fire was only a few months ago, the rubble was just hauled away," I confess, though I don't know how this is any of his business.

"And have you switched your shift? Are you still working nights at the hospital?"

"I put in the request to work first shift... Why?"

"When you get your own place, do you still plan to have that stranger stay with the kids overnight?" The intensity of his question raises the hair on the back of my neck.

"Henry, what is with the questioning?" I ask, my tone conveying my growing agitation.

"There is no need for that kind of tone, Amber. I'm trying to understand my kids' living conditions," he says in that condescending tone he developed toward the end of our marriage.

Glancing at DeeDee, she looks uncomfortable as she shifts on her feet looking anywhere but at me and my stomach sinks to my feet. Henry's up to something.

"*Our* children's living conditions are fine. We will have our own place soon." I try to sound calm in my reassurance, but it comes out flat.

"I think we should revisit the custody arrangement," Henry says and I'm sure I have gone white as a ghost. My legs feel shaky and on the verge of collapsing, and I don't even know how they are holding me up. DeeDee whips her head around, looking at Henry equally as shocked.

Once, not long after DeeDee and Henry were married, she let me know she had no plans to have children and was thrilled Henry came with kids who weren't around much. She was reassuring me in her own way, and I tried not to hold it against her, but she was Henry's mistress, so my tolerance is rather thin.

Seeing her confusion and shock only deepens the shock I'm feeling.

*This can't be happening . . ..*

I blink several times, forcing myself to take a measured breath as my heart pounds erratically against my rib cage.

Henry takes a step closer with that patronizing small smile, and I ball my fists so I don't throat-punch him. "Matt and Emily need their own space, and Matt will have more opportunities to play competitively in Kansas City than he will here in Peak Valley."

"Henry—"

He cuts me off with that dang hand of his again. "Just think about it. I'll be in touch." Before I can respond, he walks away with a shocked DeeDee, who glances over her shoulder with a worried look on her face. For the first time, she seems almost human to me.

It isn't until my heart slows to a normal beat that I realize Henry left without telling his children goodbye.

# Fight Forever

# 5

## - Luke -

"I had to gut the whole place and update the wiring and some of the plumbing. Put in central heating and air and just finished the drywall," I say to my brothers as we haul in the new kitchen cabinets.

"This place always had good bones," Eric grunts, hoisting the cabinet up to scale the steps leading into the mudroom.

"Are you planning to sell this place when its done?" Jax asks, watching Eric and me from the door he's propping open.

"I don't know," I say. Isn't that the million-dollar question? Fifteen years ago, I had planned to turn this place into a home for me and Amber. I still have hope of making this our home, but Clint's words the other night have haunted me.

*Don't you think you should move on?*

I tried moving on once. Tried to forget Amber, but there is no forgetting her. In such a short amount of time, she stole my heart. We barely had any time together before I broke us.

"Sorry I'm late," Clint says coming up the driveway. "Amber stopped by in a mood. The way she went off on me, you'd think she thought I was you." He points to me.

"What was she upset about?" I stop and set the cabinet down before it clears the back door into the mudroom where Eric is still holding up his end.

"Are you fucking kidding me?" he calls over to me. I ignore him, giving Clint my full attention.

Clint holds his hands up. "Oh, I'm not going there."

"You can't just drop a bombshell like that and not spill," Jax chimes in. He's definitely my favorite brother.

"And I like sleeping with my fiancée," Clint returns, punching Jax's arm as he passes me, picking up my abandoned end and lifting it with ease.

"Hey! Are you supposed to be lifting that?" Jax asks, releasing the door to help Clint with the cabinet.

"Probably not." Clint shrugs as he follows Eric through the mudroom into the kitchen where they put the cabinet down.

"If you don't tell me what is up with Amber, I'm going to tell Dawn you were overusing your arm," I snarl at my brother, who is rotating the shoulder that was shot several weeks ago.

"She's pissed off because her ex suggested they revisit custody," Eric says to a menacing looking Clint. "Sarah mentioned it."

"So that's where've you been." Jax gives Eric a saucy grin. "Rekindling things?"

Eric sends Jax a scathing stare. "We are working together to try to track down Darin."

Darin was Dawn's ex who got in some trouble with his biker gang and fled, leaving Dawn defenseless when they came looking for him. Now he's on the run after killing the man who shot Clint and ran Eric and Sarah off the road.

"Why is Amber's ex wanting to revisit custody?" I ask with a frown. I don't know much about Amber's ex, only that he remarried some rich socialite from Kansas City a few weeks after the divorce was finalized.

"Sarah didn't go into details, but I think it has something to do with her living with her parents," Eric says, eyeing me closely. "Sarah's asked me to look into the insurance company that denied Amber's claim."

"How can they deny her claim?"

"Usually insurance companies deny claims when there is no suspect in an arson case. When there is little proof and no suspect, they tend to believe that the property owner is responsible," Eric explains while he and Clint start moving the cabinet into position in the kitchen.

"But her house wasn't the intended target. It spread to her house," I point out, still confused that the insurance company can deny a claim so easily.

"Benny and Linda owned the house Dawn was living in. Their claim was denied as well. The insurance company is suspicious given the cause is arson and both property owners are members of the same family. To them, it looks like a family trying to commit fraud," Eric explains while I stare at him dumbfounded.

"So, there is nothing they can do?" Jax asks, looking equally perplexed.

"Sarah is working with someone in Wichita who knows insurance law to help figure out what their options are."

"And Amber's ex? He knows about the claim being denied?"

"He sells insurance. I would be surprised if he doesn't know," Clint says, rubbing the back of his neck. "She was pissed and confused. Henry's threat over custody came out of nowhere. He just told her after Matt's game this afternoon."

"Can he really take the kids from Amber because she doesn't have her own place?"

"Kansas is a mother state. I doubt a judge would want to change the kids' routine."

"But there is a chance?"

"What are you getting at, Luke?" Clint asks with shrewd eyes.

I look around, mentally prioritizing the work that would need to be done. "I have a house."

"Okay?" Jax says, tilting his head to the side in confusion.

"I have a house," I repeat, my smile stretching across my face. "And a plan."

"Don't even think about it," Clint warns but I ignore it.

I know exactly how I'm going to win Amber back.

# 6

## - Amber -

"How are you feeling, Mr. Shearson?" I ask as I walk into my patient's room to check on his vitals.

"I'd be better if you'd let me blow this joint," he grumbles while flipping through the channels.

"They plan to release you tomorrow," I confirm while looking through his chart before I go through my routine of checking his vitals and chatting him up.

Normally patients who come through the ER are scared and in a state of shock. It can be difficult and challenging, but I love it. We comfort them as we patch them up, then we send them on their way. Sometimes patients need to stay overnight for observation, like Mr. Shearson, where we monitor them. It isn't the most exciting part of the job, but I still enjoy it. I have wanted to be a nurse since I was a kid. I always thought I would work with babies, but once I started working in the ER, I knew it was where I was supposed to be.

It took me longer than I expected to get my degree, and I only landed my first job a few months ago. It has been exhausting, challenging, and more fulfilling than I ever imagined.

My only regret is not going after what I wanted sooner. I let Henry talk me into dropping out of the nursing program so I could raise Matt and help support him while he finished school and started his insurance business. I put his dream before my own, and when it was my turn to pursue my dream, Henry always had an excuse for why I shouldn't.

It wasn't until after I divorced Henry that I really started dreaming for myself again, and the first thing I did was go back to school. I was one of the oldest students and behind the curve, but I worked hard and now I'm where I am meant to be. All the stress from the late-night studying sessions, the lack of sleep from trying to get my house in order, and running the kids to all their activities was worth it because I finally get to do what I love.

"Your vitals are looking good, Mr. Shearson." I pat his shoulder and before leaving the room, I add, "Get some rest."

"Amber, good, I was looking for you," Dr. Cantana says as I walk out of Mr. Shearson's room. "I approved your shift change, but I can't move you to the new shift for another six weeks."

"Really?" I look up at him with a big smile stretching across my face. It's the first good news I have heard in weeks. I could hug the man, but that wouldn't be professional.

"Did you think I wouldn't approve it?"

"No . . . no, it's just . . . .. Thank you, Dr. Cantana, your approval means a lot," I stutter, reaching out to shake his hand.

"You'll be missed on this shift. You're a good nurse," he says with a smile and shakes my hand.

"I'm looking for Amber Baker?" I hear Luke's voice from the nurses' station a few feet ahead of me. I haven't seen or heard from him since the wedding a few weeks ago. I thought about him—a lot—and chastised myself every time I pictured running into him.

"Oh goody, it's Luke," Dr. Cantana says under his breath as we make our way down the hall to the nurses' station. The last time Luke was at the hospital he needed stitches in his hand. Searched the whole ER before he found me and waved his bloody hand at me asking if I could help him. Dr. Cantana wasn't happy, and Luke took Dr. Cantana coming to my aid as some sort of clue he was into me. Granted, I probably should have mentioned that Dr. Cantana is happily married with a kid but when it comes to Luke, I don't exactly play fair. "Luke, you can't be here, visiting hours are over."

"I'm not visiting a patient; I'm here to see Amber," Luke growls. Turning to face us, he stands several inches taller than Dr. Cantana and looks insanely territorially.

"How can I help you, Luke?" I ask before Dr. Cantana can respond. The last thing I need at my workplace is for Luke to be a jerk to Dr. Cantana… again.

"I need to talk to you." He looks away from Dr. Cantana, his warm blue eyes soften and the corners of his mouth tip up.

"Now isn't a good time." I sigh, looking down at my watch. "I have patients I need to check on."

"When do you go on lunch? Or break? They give you a break, don't they?" Luke turns his narrowed eyes on Dr. Cantana.

"Luke—"

"Go take a break, Amber." Dr. Cantana chuckles, patting Luke on the back as he passes. "Have the poor guy buy you some coffee, then check on your patients."

"I'm starting to like that guy," Luke says, pointing to Dr. Cantana with his thumb.

"C'mon, I'll take you to the cafeteria. You can buy me one coffee, but you have to promise you won't ever come to my place of work and harass me again." I sigh, walking past him toward the cafeteria, not even looking to see if he follows me.

"I wouldn't call it harassing you, but if you would give me your number, I could always call you when I need you," Luke says as he catches up with me.

"I'm not giving you my number."

"Okay then, I can't promise I won't come see you at work."

"No, Luke!" I shoot him a glare and throw my arms up in frustration. "You aren't listening to me!"

"I'm listening just fine, but you're being stubborn," he says with that smug smile of his.

"Ugh!"

"I'm not here to piss you off, but I did want to see how you were doing," Luke says and the smile on his face fades a bit as he peers down at me.

"Clint told you about the insurance claim getting denied?" I should have known it would have gotten back to Luke.

"No actually, Eric told me," Luke says with a sheepish grin as he rubs the back of his neck.

We enter the cafeteria and I lead Luke to where the coffee machines are. Grabbing a small cup, I place the cup under the French vanilla cappuccino nozzle and press the button to fill my cup. Luke walks to the only pot of black coffee and sniffs it before pouring it into his cup. The buzz from the machine is loud in the almost empty cafeteria.

Luke quickly pays for our coffee while I find us a private table in the corner. Watching him make his way to the table, he isn't just walking, he's swaggering. His warm blue eyes scan me from head to toe, and I never felt more exposed than I do now.

"What are you doing here, Luke?" I ask before he can take a seat.

"Did you know Sarah and Eric were a thing?" he counters, taking the seat opposite me.

"Yes, I knew they were a thing and no, they are not a thing now. They are just doing whatever it is single people do these days," I answer before blowing on my cappuccino to cool it down.

"You're single. Shouldn't you know what it is single people do these days?" Luke winks at me over his coffee cup, humor dancing in his eyes.

"Yes, I'm single, but I'm off the market and will be indefinitely." I roll my eyes at him and he chuckles into his coffee. "Can you *please* tell me what you want?"

"I heard about your ex," he says, looking serious as he sets his coffee cup onto the table. "I heard he was threatening to take custody."

I look away, not sure what to say. When he doesn't say anything for several seconds, I glance over at him. His eyes are on his coffee, looking conflicted before he finally looks up at me.

"Promise me you'll hear me out before you run off?"

"Excuse me?"

"I think I have a solution to your Henry problem, but I need you to promise me you'll hear me out," he says with a clenched jaw and I sense there is more he wants to say on the Henry matter but is holding back.

"Okay?"

"I mean it, Amber. I know you, now promise me you won't run and that you'll hear me out."

"Luke—"

"Promise me."

"Okay fine, I promise," I say, throwing my arms up in frustration. "I'm all ears."

"I've been working on remodeling my parents' house. Now . . . it isn't pretty on the outside, but the inside is coming together," Luke explains, but I stop him, placing a hand on his forearm.

"Did you really come here to tell me about your parents' house?"

"Well that, and to see if you would want to move into it."

*What?* "I'm sorry . . . can you repeat that?" I whisper.

"You and the kids could move into the house. Then Henry can't take custody away from you." The intensity in his eyes is so overwhelming, I have to look down at the table.

Luke always was one to step up when help was needed and here he is, offering me help even after the countless times I've pushed him away.

I tried to forget Luke over the years, but he was always there in my thoughts. I tried to hate him and for a few months, I convinced myself that I did, but really, I just hated missing him.

I was scared to see him when he first moved back to Peak Valley. Afraid that just the sight of him would hurt too much, and it did hurt seeing him smiling and more handsome than I remembered.

I knew the moment I saw him, he had the power to break me, and my heart was too scared of letting any man have that kind of power again. I pulled anger and years of sadness around me like a blanket and used it as armor.

With his offer, I don't know if he took down some of my armor or helped reinforce it. Luke knows I had so many dreams wrapped up in that house. I have no doubt its the reason he offered it to me, as a grand gesture, but I can't accept it. Not when it was meant to be our home and he took it away. How do I know he won't take it away again?

"Amber?" He looks vulnerable as he tilts his head, searching my face. "What are you thinking?"

"Um…" I clear my throat and then start over. "Thank you, Luke, its a very generous offer but I can't accept it."

"Why not?" His eyes flare for a moment before he wracks a hand through his hair. "Is it because I'm offering?"

"No," I lie, but the way his eyes narrow at me, I know he knows I'm lying. "I can't afford to pay rent on a house that size and pay my mortgage."

"Who said you would have to pay rent?" Luke sounds defensive before he reaches over and wraps his hands around both of mine, which are still holding my cappuccino. The heat from the coffee is nothing compared to the heat that floods my system whenever Luke touches me. "The house is paid off… has been for years. I'm trying to offer you help, Amber. I don't understand why you won't take it."

"My parents, Dawn, and Clint are all helping me in ways I can't even begin to pay back," I say, looking deep into Luke's warm eyes, hoping I don't get lost in them as I try to make him understand. "I have my pride. I've worked really hard to be able to stand on my own two feet, and its important to me to work for what I have and need. I can't accept your offer. It feels too much like a handout."

Luke doesn't say anything for several long seconds. The intensity of his stare is too much for me, so I look at where he's wrapped his hands around mine. His hands are warm and callused, larger than mine. My dad always said a man's hands say a lot about a man, and I know Luke's hands speak of his hard work.

"The house still needs a lot of work. What if you helped me with the remodel?" he offers quietly, the laughter that is normally in his voice gone. "In exchange for living there."

"Luke—"

"Just think about it." He sighs and releases my hands. Not even the heat from the coffee can fight off the cold absence of his touch. Standing from his chair, he peers down at me with remorse-filled blue eyes. I want to stand and let him wrap me up in a hug like he used to and take away the pain, but I don't let myself move from my chair, and I don't watch him walk away.

## Fight Forever

When my shift ends, I drive home to find my mom waiting at the kitchen table with a cup of coffee and a thick envelope addressed to me from the Johnson County Courthouse. I don't need to read it to know what it is.

# 7

# - Luke -

After a week of radio silence, I was ready to abandon my plan to move Amber and her kids into my old home and think of a new strategy.

Almost immediately, I knew offering the house to her wasn't a grand gesture but a ripping of old wounds. I was an idiot for thinking she would want to live in the house I promised to turn into her dream home.

"Luke?"

*I must be dreaming.*

"Amber?" I call from atop the ladder I'm on inside my shop I purchased for my construction business.

"Is it safe to come in?" she asks from the entrance door.

"Yeah." I grin like a fool at her. Amber is here in my shop, and I didn't have to do any scheming to get her here.

"Can we talk?" she asks, fidgeting with her purse strap. She's looking sexy in her scrubs and her hair is pulled into a bun on top of her head. This is the last place she wants to be, but I push that thought aside.

"Yeah, give me a sec," I say, clipping my nail gun to my toolbelt and climb down the ladder. "We can talk in my office."

"In there?" She points to the tiny house I'm working on, her eyes wide.

"No, darlin', I have a real office in the back." I chuckle, taking off my toolbelt and setting it down. "Want some coffee?"

"Sure?" She hesitates before falling in step with me as we move toward the back of the shop. "Dawn said you were starting a construction company. Why are you working on a mini house?"

"The realtor I worked with to buy this shop asked if I could build him a tiny house to put on some property he owns in northwestern Kansas. He likes to hunt and wants to bring his family. It'll keep me busy through the winter months until I can pick up some more clients." I watch as she takes in all the machinery, tools, and material laid out around the shop. I'm not the kind of guy who needs validation, but I need Amber's. I need her to see I'm a safe bet; God knows I've screwed up one too many times with her. If I'm going to win her back, I have to prove to her that I can be the man she once fell in love with.

"I only have black coffee." I cringe, holding the office door open for her.

"Black is fine." She glances around the office before taking a seat in one of the ratty chairs Dawn purchased at a garage sale.

I feel her eyes follow me to the coffee machine behind my desk. Never one to be intimidated, but I know how she is scrutinizing my every move right now. I need to tread lightly. She's here for a reason—hopefully to accept my offer—and if I scare her away now, I may not get another opportunity.

"I got to hang out with Matt the other day," I say and hand her a cup of coffee, praying she doesn't notice it's a few hours old.

"He said you taught him how to hit a curveball."

"Didn't have to do much teaching; he's a natural." I take a seat on my desk across from her, letting my legs stretch out between her.

"He gets his athleticism from me."

"He gets all his good traits from you." I flash a flirty smile, though I mean it. Matt and Emily were at Dawn and Clint's apartment after school while Amber was at parent/teacher conferences. Jax came over and we went out to the back of the shop and hit a few baseballs. I had fun hanging out with Matt. He has Amber's eyes, just like his sister, and he has her wit. He's more serious than Amber, but I suspect that comes from being the only man in the house.

"I enjoyed hanging out with him."

She eyes me curiously before uncertainty mars her features. "What are those?" She points to the wall behind my desk where blueprints are tacked up.

"Can you keep a secret?"

"Yes?"

"I mean it. You can't tell anyone about it or I'm a dead man."

"Well, in that case, please tell me," she says with sarcasm and a ghost of a smile.

"They're blueprints for a house Clint plans to build on the north end of his property. He's giving the blueprints to Dawn as a wedding present," I share, and her eyes brighten with happiness that wasn't there when she first arrived.

"Dawn is going to be so surprised!" A dreamy look appears on her face for a moment. A kernel of insight into Amber's dreams—dreams I want to be a part of.

"I'm going to be the contractor on the build," I say as I turn to look at the blueprints then back at her.

"That's good." She nods then looks down at her hands which fist in her lap. "I wanted to see if the offer you made is still an option?"

"Yes." I sit my coffee mug down and lean forward. "Are you accepting?"

"Yes." She sighs and looks up at me with a brave face. I take a good look at her. She looks exhausted and worry lines crease her brow. Something's happened and it's stressing her out.

"What's going on?" I ask. Not meaning to, I cup my hands around her face, tilting it toward me. I fight the urge to pull her into a bear hug and tell her whatever her troubles are, I'm here for her. She used to love my bear hugs, but I don't think she'd appreciate it now. Not yet.

She stares at me, surprised, for several seconds before putting her hands on mine and gently pushing them. It stings, but I force myself to sit back on the desk, planting my hands on the edge.

"I need to move in before Christmas. Do you think that is possible?"

"That's what, six weeks away?" I mentally calculate in my head as I go through all the work that still needs to be done in the house. "The inside of the house can be finished, but the exterior will be tough."

"I don't need it to look pretty; I just need it to be livable and not dangerous or hazardous." She looks defeated with her shoulders slumped. I hate not being able to reassure her. "My parents and I will help with whatever we can."

I nod, watching her, though she looks anywhere but at me. "What happened?"

"I just need a place for the kids to have their own space. When do you think we can move in?"

"I can have the kitchen done by the end of the week. Do you want to help with painting this weekend? Once the paint is done, you should be able to move in. The bathrooms need work, but they function. We can work on those while you live there. Does that sound okay?" I run my hands through my hair.

"We can move in before Thanksgiving?" Surprise and maybe a little bit of relief soften the stress lines and a surge of pride warms my chest.

"Yes." I nod, wanting to do more. She's carrying so much weight on her shoulders that she looks close to crumbling. "You're not telling me something."

"I just need the kids in a home with their own space."

"I'm not asking for a watered-down version. I want to know why you look as if there is no light at the end of the tunnel you're stuck in."

Amber takes in a deep breath. Leaning forward, she rests her elbows on her knees and smooths back her hair. "Henry is coming after me pretty hard. I've got to get into a house and establish a history of stability before the custody hearing."

"Establish a history of stability? Is that in question?"

"Henry put together a laundry list of instabilities and neglect claims from leaving the kids with strangers to not providing adequate educational resources." She lets her head fall into her hands.

I stare at the floor, my teeth grinding together. I can't afford to lose my temper in front of Amber, not now when she swallowed the last of her pride to share those painful details.

Frowning, I cross my arms over my chest and make a mental note to have Eric look into Amber's ex. Something about her ex coming after her and the suddenness of it rubs me the wrong way. And from what I have seen, she's a great mother and her kids seem to be thriving. Matt nor Emily have shown any signs of neglect and as a kid who was neglected, I would have been able to see the signs.

"Sorry," I finally say after several seconds of silence.

She shrugs on an exhale. "It's not your fault."

"I know, but I'm still sorry you have to go through this. Is there anything I can do?"

"I just need the house," she says quietly.

"When is the hearing?"

"Sarah was able to get the motion hearing moved to Peak Valley, and due to the holidays, she has pushed it back until the end of January," Amber explains and I've never been more thankful that Amber's sister is a lawyer than I am in this moment.

"I can have it move-in ready by the end of this week," I state. Pushing the timeline will be hard, but possible with some help. Thankfully, Jax is still in town, and with help from Clint, and maybe even Amber's dad, it shouldn't be difficult. "There won't be any furniture, but that shouldn't stop you from moving in, right?"

"No, I can work on furnishing it after we move in."

"I have some of my parents' old furniture you can use if you need."

"Thanks. So, painting this weekend?" Amber pulls her phone from her purse and she brings up a calendar. "I work Friday night, and Matt has a game Saturday morning, but I can help paint after the game."

"Perfect, send me what colors you want for the kids' room and for your room."

"Just paint them whatever you're painting the rest of the house." She waves off, still scrolling through her phone.

"I don't want to paint the walls a generic color. I want to make it a home."

"I'll talk to the kids and get back with you." She rolls her eyes and I flash her a triumphant smile.

"Can you have a six-month lease contract written up in the next couple of days? Or do you want something shorter or longer?"

I slit my eyes at her. "No contract."

"Why not?"

"Because I know nothing about contracts." I sigh, running a hand down my face. "Why does it have to be so *official*? Can't it be two friends working together?"

"Friends?"

"Well, it would be easier working together if we were friends." Because friendship with Amber is getting a foot in the door and one step closer to winning her back.

Now would be a good time to tell her I plan to live there too, but the words don't come out. She's moving in and I don't want to risk her changing her mind.

"I have two kids I need to think about. I can't move them in only for you to change your mind and kick us out. I need some sort of assurance that you won't disrupt our lives, at least until this whole custody thing blows over."

"You really think I would do that to you?"

"No." She looks away, embarrassment blushing her cheeks. "Sorry, that was mean."

"You're forgiven, but let's not make this harder than it needs to be. The place is yours until you don't want it anymore."

"Thank you, Luke." She smiles at me and with those three words, I have hope again.

# Fight Forever

# 8

## - Amber -

I watch my parents and kids follow Luke into the house. Their excited chatter fades when they shut the red front door. It isn't the same red door from fifteen years ago; this one is newer, more modern, and exactly what I would have picked out.

*Am I really doing this?*

Looking up at the house that held so many hopes and dreams, I mentally try to prepare myself. These last few days have been such a whirlwind trying to prepare me and the kids for the move, that I never stopped to think about how I might feel once I finally walk through the front door.

"What are we staring at?" Burns asks, coming to stand next to me, his wrinkled face scrunched in contemplation.

"Burns, hi, thanks for coming to help." I kiss his cheek.

"I ain't here to help, I'm here to watch my boys paint Emily's room pink sparkles," he says, returning the kiss to my cheek before holding up a dated Polaroid camera. "I'm getting it all on camera to use against them when they piss me off."

"I want copies." I point at him, then pat his shoulder as he heads for the front door.

"You comin'?" He thumbs toward the house.

I wave him on. "In a minute."

The house is still drab looking with its peeling paint and cracked concrete steps, but it's still a beautiful house. Just rough around the edges. I want to hate it, but no matter how hard I look for fault in this house, I find nothing that would justify bailing on this place. Unless you count having an insanely hot landlord as a reason . . . .. At least I don't have to deal with him all the time. In fact, our paths shouldn't cross that often, and I can just avoid him when he needs to work on the house.

"What are we staring at?" Dawn asks. I should really go inside. Everyone probably thinks I'm losing my mind, standing out here all alone just staring at my new home.

"Nothing," I mutter, rubbing my temples. "Tell me this is a good idea."

"It's a good idea," Dawn says, nodding her head with a teasing smile.

"It's a terrible idea," Clint says, coming to stand next to his fiancée. He wraps an arm around her shoulders and looks at me. "I still can't believe you're moving in with Luke."

"I'm not moving in with Luke," I deny. "He's my landlord, that's it."

"Where's he living, then?"

"I don't . . .. Oh no." Realization dawns on me and I storm up the steps, through the front door, and scan the room for my intended target. "Lucas Michael Colson!"

"Oh shit." Luke swallows when he sees how furious I am.

A camera snaps with a flash before Burns pulls the Polaroid from the camera, laughing.

"You *live* here?"

"Amber—"

"Don't you think you should have mentioned that?" I all but scream at him. This is bad, very, very bad. I can't live with Luke. Not in this house. Not in any house.

"Maybe you guys should have this little chat elsewhere?" my mother says cautiously.

"Luke is living with us?" Emily asks, her toothless smile wide across her face. "Yay!"

"No, he is *not* living with us!"

"Can we take this outside?" Luke asks as he runs his hand over his short-cropped hair, not a trace of guilt found on his face. No, he looks amused. *Amused!*

"Might as well duke it out here, we'll just eavesdrop on you both," Burns says, still holding his camera, ready to capture the drama.

"Shut it, old man," Luke growls and Burns snaps another picture.

"I can't believe you didn't tell me!"

"I thought you knew." He shrugs.

"Liar!"

"Okay, yes, but—"

"You son of a motherless goat!" I cry out, raising my arms in frustration.

"We're taking this outside." Luke moves faster than I can dodge him, grabbing my elbow and leading me out the front door, down the cracked porch steps to the middle of the lawn, away from inquiring minds and the photo frenzy.

I point at him. "This deal is off!"

"No, it's not."

"Yes, it is, Luke!"

"You're going to go tell Emily she can't have her pink sparkle room, and Matt can't have his Jayhawks-themed room?" Luke cocks his head with a smug grin I want to smack off his gorgeous face.

He's got me there. The kids are excited about moving here. Matt has a friend who lives two doors down and is looking forward to riding the bus with him.

"No . . .."

"Good—"

"Wait, Jayhawks theme?" I scrunch my nose. "Matt wants a Jayhawks, as in a KU Jayhawks-themed room?"

"Yeah, your mom texted about painting an accent wall and putting up a large wall sticker."

"You're *texting* with my mom now? What else aren't you telling me?" I tap my foot. My traitorous mother . . . I should have known she would somehow butt her nose into this.

"I'm not texting your mom." I shoot him a glare. "Okay, maybe I'm texting your mom, but only because I thought you were being stubborn and not texting me yourself."

"I wasn't being stubborn. I didn't know Matt had told my mom about wanting a KU theme. I thought he just wanted to paint his room red."

"Amber, I'm sorry I didn't tell you I was living here," Luke says, though he doesn't look sorry at all. He takes a step into my personal space; his hand lightly slides down my arm and a shiver that has nothing to do with the late autumn air tracks down my spine. "I've got a lot of work to do in this house. I'm going to be here all the time as it is. Is this really going to be an issue?"

"I don't know," I groan, covering my face with my hands. "What if Henry finds out?"

"Why do you care if he finds out?" Luke growls and pulls my hands away from my face. He inches closer to me and I have to tilt my head up just to see his face.

"It will be more ammunition for him to use against me," I confess, completely aware of his closeness but not wanting to move away. I find comfort in his closeness. When he's close, just for a moment, I feel like some of the burden I carry is lifted. It's the kind of comfort I could get used to, but a luxury I can't afford.

"Talk to Sarah. If she thinks Henry can use it against you, I'll move out. But if she thinks it's fine, will you promise me something?"

"What?" I whisper, caught up in the intensity of his eyes.

"Stop fighting me and let me help you."

"I'm not promising you that."

"We're friends now, remember? Friends help each other. Stop being so stubborn."

"Fine, I'll talk to Sarah. But if you do anything inappropriate that jeopardizes the custody hearing, I'm gone."

"If I do anything that jeopardizes the hearing, you won't have to move out, I will." Luke says it like a promise, and I believe him, even though he broke so many promises to me long ago.

*****

"So, day three of living with Luke . . ..
Spill." Dawn is hanging out with me in my master
bedroom bathroom. I didn't want the master
bedroom, but Luke insisted. The two kids are
upstairs in rooms that share a Dick and Jane
bathroom, and Luke is in the guest bedroom down
the hall from mine.

I called Sarah as soon as we finished
painting and told her about Luke's scheming. I
expected her to take my side, but all she did was
laugh for a solid straight minute before giving
kudos to Luke for his sly antics. I was pissed, and
not happy to hear that Sarah didn't think it would
be an issue, especially since Luke and his brother
Clint were close family friends. She even thought
having Luke around to testify to my stellar
parenting skills would help. *Help!* Not at all what I
was expecting.

It's official now. I'm moved into my old
dream house with my ex-boyfriend. I really didn't
see this coming.

Tonight is the first night I'm leaving the
kids overnight in the house with Luke while I
work. I'm not exactly comfortable leaving the kids

with Luke. Not because I think he won't take good care of them. No, it's the opposite. They love having him around. They are growing attached. Matt has been Luke's little apprentice, helping with projects around the house, and Emily is convinced he's her personal cuddling giant.

"Do men always walk around shirtless? Henry never did but I mean, its freezing outside and Luke walks around in nothing but gym shorts. Matt's starting to do it, too," I complain as I put on a few coats of mascara.

"I'm pretty sure he's doing that on purpose." Dawn giggles as she hands me my lip gloss and takes the mascara to put away.

"Well, if he's trying to seduce me, it won't work. I am closed for business," I mutter. I had a feeling Luke's shirtless shenanigans were an attempt to drive me wild with desire, and I hate to admit that it's working. It doesn't help that he is always super attentive and helpful.

"What's that look?"

"What look?" I try to play dumb, but she knows me too well.

"That goofy grin, dreamy-eyed look. I don't think you are closed for business at all."

"I'm so closed for business, I'm no longer operational." I smirk at her through the mirror.

"I used to think that, but Clint was able to get me up and running again. Now I'm having his baby." She looks through the small makeup collection I have when she asks, "Why not go for it? I mean he's willing, he likes you. A lot. What's so wrong with giving Luke a shot?"

I nibble my lip, not exactly sure how to answer her.

"You're being stubborn."

"I'm not being stubborn." I frown at her. "I swore off men. All men."

"Why?"

"Between Luke and Henry, I've learned my lesson."

"So, because of Luke and Henry, you are never going to dip your toe into the dating pool?" she asks, unconvinced.

"Exactly."

She blinks at me. "That makes no sense."

"It makes perfect sense." I smack my lips together, then dab on some more lip gloss.

"I think you're scared. I don't think you learned any lesson; you're just flat-out scared." I open my mouth to say something, but she continues, "Luke knows you, and he's going to do the pushy Colson thing."

"He can try."

"I think he's one step ahead of you." She laughs and hops off the bathroom counter.

*Frick . . . . She may be right.*

# Fight Forever

# 9

## - Luke -

"Luke!" Emily comes flying into my room. I love having the kids and Amber under my roof. It's been a whole week, and I haven't been this happy in a long time. There were a few adjustments, but nothing major. I have to be mindful of little ears but that's no biggie. Amber's taught me a few colorful replacements.

Amber is still trying to keep me at arm's length, but I'm wearing her down. I caught her watching me with hunger in her eyes just the other day. I need to be patient and keep showing her I can be a partner; someone she can rely on.

"I can't find my shoes." Emily jumps up and down in front of me. She may also need to use the restroom. I don't know, I don't speak six-year-old. *Yet.* But I'm learning.

"Where did you put them last?" I smile down at her, thankful I'm dressed no less.

"On my feet." She looks down. "Now they are gone!"

"Okay . . .." I'm not sure how that could have happened, but I can handle this, I think. "Let's go on a hunt for your shoes."

"But I've looked everywhere," she whines with a frown, slumping her little shoulders. Is this what a tantrum looks like? Or do they get worse than this?

"Well, I guess we have to look again."

"Okay," she huffs and runs out of the room as quickly as she barreled in.

"Matt! Hurry up or you'll be late!" Amber calls up the stairs while I'm coming down the hallway following Speedy Gonzales Emily. Even without makeup, worn jeans, and a sweatshirt with her son's basketball team logo, she's positively divine. Gorgeous in a way that turns me into a horny teenage boy.

I brush up close beside her and smile when I hear her intake a sharp breath. I'm not even shirtless. *Winning.*

"I'm coming!" Matt responds, zooming down the stairs with his bag on one arm and his shoes in the other. "Where is my hoodie?"

"It should be in your closet where it belongs," Amber says, trying to ignore me.

"Morning," I say close to her ear and watch her shiver.

"Luke, are you coming to my game? It's the last one of the season." Matt plops on the stairs to put on his shoes.

"Sure am, bud." I smile and ruffle his hair, maneuvering around him. "Your hoodie is on the kitchen table."

"Awesome!"

"You're coming?" Amber looks up at me. Apparently, Matt neglected to tell her.

"Yeah, Matt invited me last night." I shrug, flashing a coy smile.

"Luke, I still can't find my shoes!" Emily hollers from her room.

"I'm coming." Amber sighs, heading up the stairs.

I wave her off. "I got this."

"Luke—"

"Here," I toss her my keys, "load Matt in my truck, I'll get Emily."

Amber tosses the keys back to me. "Your truck doesn't have Emily's booster."

"So, put it in." I toss them back. "We can get lunch after the game, then look at furniture. We are going to need furniture if we're hosting Thanksgiving."

"We are?"

"That's what Clint said."

"Why am I always the last to know everything?" Amber groans and storms off. Matt chuckles as he follows her.

"Found them!" Emily shouts from the top of the stairs, holding her shoes up triumphantly. I'm starting to think she only has one volume level, loud.

"Where were they, little human?" I ask in my giant voice that makes her giggle.

"In my closet," she says, tugging one on, then sticking her foot out for me to tie her shoe.

I take her foot and tie up the laces. "Don't you know how to tie a shoe?"

"Yep, but you do it better." She smiles at me and lifts her other shoe.

"Lazy little human." I narrow my eyes at her, tying the other shoe. "You tricked me."

"Nah-uh." She giggles.

"Come on, let's move." I pick her up and tickle her all the way to the truck.

*****

"You didn't have to come," Amber whispers softly in my ear as we take our seats in the stands.

"I wouldn't miss it, even if it means putting up with your grumpy ass," I whisper back.

"You aren't supposed to cuss, Luke," Emily says from Amber's lap, not looking up from her tablet. "Are giants allowed to cuss, Mommy?"

"No, they aren't."

"Sorry, little human, I won't cuss again," I giant grumble to her, then scoot in close to Amber. I want every man in this gymnasium to know Amber's mine.

"Amber?" a man I've never seen before calls up from the court floor and I almost put my arm around her when she stiffens. This must be Henry. He's wearing an expensive suit and his face is pinched as if he smelled something bad. "A word."

"Can it wait until after the game? It's about to start." She points to the clock. The boys are already starting to get into their positions.

Henry narrows his eyes at her, pressing his lips together, then looks at Emily. "Emily come with me," Henry orders, holding his hand out and waving for her to come.

"Mommy, do I have to?" Emily looks up at her mom, her emerald eyes bright with fear. I clench my fists so I don't snatch her up so this douchebag can't have her.

"You don't get to see your dad that often. You should sit with him and DeeDee."

"DeeDee couldn't make it," Henry says, looking impatient. The referees are eyeing Henry, waiting for him to move so they can start the game. "Emily, don't make me come up there."

Amber pastes on a fake, reassuring smile as she lifts Emily from her lap. "Take your tablet and show your dad the new spelling game you are so good at."

"Emily, I'm not going to let you play on your tablet if you keep disobeying me," Henry spits out loud enough to carry across the stands. Other parents turn to watch.

"Go on, Emily." Amber's hands shake when she nudges Emily toward the stairs. I'm blocking Emily's way but don't move. I can't move. I don't want to watch Emily be forced to do something she's scared to do. I want to protect her and scare away her fears, but what choice do I have? I'm not her father, and Henry has a right to see Emily.

Emily looks to me with a plea in her eyes—eyes that are so much like her mother's. My gut twists and I still refuse to move. Decision made, I'm not going to let this man take her unless she wants to go.

I lean in close and ask, "Do you want to go with him?" Two small arms dart around my neck and hold on tight.

"I don't want to go with him. Please, Luke, can I stay with you?" Emily pleads in my ear and I wrap her in my arms. No one is taking her, not without force.

"Emily, stop being a baby and come here," Henry hisses as he moves up the stairs. My hand runs down Emily's hair while Amber rubs Emily's back, who looks visibly upset and uncertain.

"Touch her and I'll break your hand," I growl. Henry recoils

"Excuse me?" His lip curls with disgust before shifting his glare to Amber.

"She wants to stay with her mom, and I don't think you want to continue to force your daughter to come with you. Not in front of all these witnesses. It's the kind of scene that won't end well for you," I say quietly enough that others around us can't hear. "Now, the game is starting, and I think you need to go sit somewhere else. Let Emily calm down and maybe if she wants to come sit with you, Amber will bring her over."

"Amber, who the hell is this guy?"

"He's right, Henry, you're making a scene. Go sit down," Amber says to my relief. I don't know what I would have done if Amber told me I had to let Emily go.

Henry opens his mouth to say something but thinks better and promptly snaps it shut before he turns to leave.

As soon as he is out of earshot, I turn to Amber, who slumps her shoulders. "So, that's the ex?"

"Yep, and it's not the last we've heard from him." She sighs, looking worried.

Before I can say anything, a whistle blows, signaling the start of Matt's game, and Amber's focus shifts.

"I love you, Giant Luke." Emily sniffs in my ear and my heart breaks a little. It breaks for Emily and Matt. No one should be scared of their father. I've been that kid and hurt for them. They don't deserve it.

# Fight Forever

# 10

## - Amber -

"Are you sure it's a good idea for the kids to go with Henry?" Luke asks again, watching Henry load them up in his car.

"He's their father, he has a right to spend time with them," I try to reassure him, though he only frowns at me.

"They didn't even want to go," he grumbles as he climbs into the truck. "Are they always like that?"

"They sometimes resist, but I think it's because they don't see him that often." I try to justify their actions, but the truth is, I have been concerned lately. They've resisted seeing Henry more than usual these last few months, and when they return home, they are distant and quiet.

"Do you think he's hurting them?"

"Not physically." I sigh because I don't think Henry would do anything to hurt them physically. Henry's criticisms cut deep, though. "His words aren't always nice, but mostly, I think he's absent. Even when he has them for his weekends, he is always working or has some event he has to attend. From what Matt has told me, they are with a babysitter a lot."

"Emily seemed scared."

"Henry doesn't understand kids and thinks they should be little adults, and Emily's tender heart doesn't understand."

"He has no business having custody," Luke snarls and starts the engine. "I'm starving, how about Mexican?"

"We don't need to go out. I'll eat the leftovers and I need a nap. I don't want to mess up my sleep schedule."

"Let me feed you, then we can take a nap," Luke says, turning down Main Street, going in the opposite direction of our house.

"I'm not napping with you." I slit my eyes at him.

"I'm great at cuddling. Just ask Emily."

"Not happening."

"Food it is. You can fill up on chips and salsa, and I'll eat the rest of your shrimp quesadillas you can't finish."

"Who says I can't finish them?"

"Experience." Luke chuckles, shooting a wink at me.

"Yeah, well, a lot has changed since we last had Mexican food together," I grumble, not entirely happy about sharing a meal *alone* with Luke Colson. It's bad enough we live under the same roof where he doesn't mind walking around without a shirt, making all my lady parts light up and my defenses falter, but now I have to share a meal with him, without the kids as a buffer.

"Someday you're going to have to tell me all about those changes," Luke says with a wolfish grin.

"Never going to happen." I try to sound firm, but his playfulness always breaks through my barriers. He could always get people to relax with his playful banter. Turn a foe into a best friend and has been working that charm on me.

"C'mon, I want to know. I want to know everything about you. Leave nothing out."

"Well, I don't want you to know any more than you need to know," I groan, closing my eyes as I let my head fall back onto the headrest.

"As your roommate, I think it's my right to know about your past. For all I know, you could have become a professional pen thief. Nurses are always needing pens . . .. Tell me, Amber, are you stealing other nurses' pens?"

"No, I'm not stealing anyone's pens! Ugh! You are driving me nuts."

"You're grumpy when you're tired." Luke yawns. "Come on, quick lunch, then you can nap." Luke puts his truck into park outside the local Mexican restaurant, *La Hacienda*.

"Fine, a quick bite but no monkey business," I grumble and climb out of his truck.

"Where is the fun in that?"

We enter the restaurant and Luke tells the hostess lunch for two. She promptly pulls two menus and leads us to a booth in the back. There are several people I know here, and all of them watch us.

I have no doubt news has spread far and wide of our new living arrangement, but it's the assumptions everyone is making that concerns me.

"Your waitress will be here shortly with your chips and to take your drink orders." The hostess smiles, puts our menus down, and walks away.

"Everyone is looking at us," I whisper to Luke.

"Let them. I want everyone to know you are off-limits." He smiles, not looking at me but reading through the menu.

"I'm off-limits because I choose to be off-limits . . . not because I'm with you." I narrow my eyes at him.

"For now." He shrugs, then puts the menu down. "I'm getting the fajitas. Shrimp quesadillas?"

"What's that supposed to mean?"

"It was a question. Are you getting shrimp quesadillas?" He cocks his head at me, biting back a chuckle.

"No, the 'for now' part," I hiss, but before I can tell him we will never get back together, the waitress arrives.

She sets down the chips and salsa, and then takes our drink and lunch order before rushing off almost as quickly as she came.

"Do you think we can go shopping for living room furniture tomorrow, or will it mess with your sleep?"

"Why do you ignore everything I tell you?" I lean in and mutter at him. "It's annoying."

"I don't ignore everything, I just disregard most of it." He chuckles, shoving a chip into his mouth.

"Can you please be serious for one moment?"

"Absolutely. I think we should go on a date," he says, then shoves another chip into his mouth.

"No."

"Why not?"

"Because I don't date," I huff and lean back in the booth seat, but only for a second. Luke's eating all the chips and salsa, and they are my favorite.

"Fine, we can just skip the dating and go straight into a relationship."

"I hate you," I say around the chip in my mouth.

"You don't. You want to hate me, but you can't." My heart skips a beat. There is more truth in his words than I care to admit.

Luke watches me and a smile plays across his face. He's doing that thing where he reads my thoughts as if I'm an open book, but I'm not an open book. I'm closed up tight, yet he keeps prying me open and taking peeks inside. He won't stop until he's written our ending.

"Furniture shopping tomorrow afternoon will work. I can sleep most of the day while the kids hang out with my parents."

"Who is ignoring who now?" He smirks but continues before I can comment, "Let me watch the kids. I want to get to know them better."

"I can't ask you to do that," I say nibbling on a chip.

"Come on, it'll be fun. I want to help. This way you can sleep and not worry about getting them ready and lugging them to your parents. It's a win-win situation."

"For whom?" I scoff and he chuckles. "What's so funny?"

"You are adorable when you are riled up."

My stomach flutters and I look away so he can't see my cheeks flush, but nothing gets past Luke.

"Sexy and beautiful," he whispers, leaning in close. "I bet you taste better than I remember."

I narrow my eyes at him. "Stop messing with me."

"I'm not messing with you. I mean every word. You're the one who is being stubborn."

"I'm not being stubborn."

"Really?" He arches a skeptical brow at me. "Give me one good reason why you won't go on a date with me."

"I . . . I don't have to."

"See, stubborn."

"You want a reason." I lace my fingers over the table and stare at him. "Because I don't trust you."

"Fair enough." He nods but doesn't look away. "I've got some explaining to do."

"I don't need you to explain anything to me. Let's just be friends and leave it at that." I did not mean for the conversation to lead us here, and I'm not sure I'm ready for an explanation.

Fortunately for me, our food arrives and Luke digs in. We sit mostly in silence while we eat and despite all my efforts, I can't eat all of my quesadillas. Luke gobbles it up with an *I told you* so smirk.

When the check is dropped off, Luke swipes it and refuses to let me see it or pay half, claiming he ate the majority of the food so he should pay.

"I'm just saying that I can pay for my own meal," I grumble as we leave the restaurant.

"I know you can pay; I just don't want you to pay."

"You can't always be calling the shots, Luke. That's now how this works." I glare over at him when we arrive at the truck.

Luke doesn't walk to the driver's side of the truck, but instead, he follows me to the passenger side. He steps in close, pinning me against the truck. His chest is in my direct line of vision and I have to tilt my head up to see him. There is something in his eyes that sends tingles to places I don't want tingles. "So, we are a 'this'?"

"That's not what I meant." My voice sounds breathy and my heart picks up. The winter air does nothing to stop the heat creeping up my neck.

"Amber?" The way he says my name causes my lungs to freeze.

"Y-yes," I choke out as he dips his head toward mine and my eyes flutter shut.

"Can I get the door for you?" he whispers over my lips and my eyes pop open.

Luke steps back a little but not by much, and I can see the laughter in his smile. Reaching for the door handle, he beeps the locks and I shove him hard. "I hate you."

"I think we just established that you don't."

# 11

## - Luke -

"Hey, little humans," I say, opening the door.

"Did you have fun?" Amber smiles brightly, hugging Matt then Emily as they enter.

Neither says a word and the hair on the back of my neck prickles. Henry takes a step into the house, and I grip the door hard so I don't slam it in his face.

"Tell your father thank you and say goodbye," Amber instructs with no sign of animosity.

"Can I speak with you?" Henry asks, not interested in hugs goodbye from his kids. They don't seem eager either, not moving from their mother's side. "Alone." He glances at me with disdain.

"Sure," Amber says with uncertainty and a flash of anxiety washes over her beautiful face when she looks at me.

"Kids, why don't you head upstairs? We'll be up in a sec." I nod for them to go with a reassuring smile.

Emily takes Matt's hand, and he leads her to the stairs. There is fear in his eyes when he glances between his mom and Henry. I mentally note to talk to Amber more about the fear the kids have. It isn't normal.

I was once in Matt's shoes when I was a kid, living in fear of my father. He was a drunk, mean bastard. There was a time when I loved him, but then it turned into hate and resentment. I'd give anything for Matt and Emily not to have to go through that, but it's not my place to step in. All I can do is support Amber and be there for the kids—the same way Burns was there for me and my brothers.

"You have no right to order my kids around," Henry hisses before the kids are out of earshot.

"Henry—"

"Now I need to speak to Amber, alone." He curls his lip at me.

My resolve snaps and I move into Henry's space, and for just a moment, he looks terrified. Good, maybe a taste of his own medicine will change his ways. "At no point will you ever be alone with Amber. Given that there is a pending hearing for custody, anything you need to say can be done in writing."

"Do you think I'm going to allow you to stay here with my children?" He must have been questioning the kids during lunch about me if he already knows about our living situation.

"I think it's none of your business where Luke stays." Amber steps in, her soft touch on my forearm relaxes some of the tension in my shoulders. I take a step back; Amber needs to fight this battle. As much as I want to intervene, she needs to let Henry know he can't push her around.

"You want to fuck any man who gives you a little bit of attention, that's your right. But I don't want them in my kids' life, got it?" Henry snaps, pointing his figure in Amber's face. Never mind,

I'm ending this now. No man should ever talk to a woman like that, especially the mother of their children.

I move to get in Henry's face, but Amber blocks me. "You diddled with women who gave you a little bit of attention *while* we were married, and you moved in with DeeDee before we were divorced. You had no problem introducing *her* to the kids without running it by me. I'm just following your lead." Amber is calm and looks bored, only angering Henry more. He fumes for a moment and looks ready to say something, but Amber cuts him off, "I think it's time for you to leave, Henry. You can email me whatever it is you wanted to say."

Amber grabs the door and starts to shut it, forcing Henry to step back. "This isn't over," he snarls and Amber pauses.

"That's where you're wrong, Henry. You aren't going to win custody, no matter how poorly you paint me in court. Those kids have no relationship with you, and they love living in Peak Valley. So, whatever game you're trying to play, end it now because you're going to lose." Before Henry can say another word, Amber slams the door and I wish I could see his face.

Amber spins around to face me with a bright smile. "God, that felt good!"

I'm not sure what possessed me to push her up against the door, but my mouth devours hers, pinning her in place and tasting the sweetness of her lips.

Were they always this soft? She sucks in a surprised breath and I dive in, taking ownership of her mouth, worshipping it. Amber's hands fist my shirt then she shoves me. Hard.

"Lucas Michael Colson!" She shoves me again, her breath coming out in pants.

"Standing up to Henry was *sexy*." I smile coyly at her, the flush in her cheeks and wildness in her emerald eyes makes my dick twitch. I almost go in for seconds.

"Don't you dare," she warns, reading my mind.

"I thought we were having a moment." I wink, shoving my hands into my pockets and stepping back to give her space but damn, I love it when she gets worked up.

"We were until you ruined it by acting like a caveman," she chastises. Amber steps away from the door and moves toward the stairs, unable to hide her smile.

I turn to face her. "Get used to it."

"Never going to happen again." She waves over her back as she ascends the stairs.

*Oh, it's going to happen again.*

\*\*\*\*\*

"This is the one you want?" I ask, staring at the plain black leather sectional. It doesn't remotely look like something she would want in the house—it's more of a bachelor pad style.

"I didn't say it's what I wanted; I said it would work well in your space." Amber rolls her eyes. I know what she's trying to do and it isn't going to work. She can be stubborn all she wants, but I will fill that house with all the furniture she loves.

"What do you want?"

"I don't know." She shrugs but her eyes drift toward a turquoise sectional set with dark-colored end tables and crystal lamps.

"Let's check that out." I nod to it and grab her hand. She tries to jerk it away, but I hold on tight.

"I want to hold Luke's hand, too!" Emily says as she grabs my free hand.

114

"As you wish, little human." I smile at her and she gives me a scrunched nose smile. It's a smile she's been giving me lately, and I think it's supposed to mean something but I'm still learning little girl speak so I have no idea what. Matt wanted to hang out with a friend who lives down the street, so it's just me and my girls looking at furniture.

"What do you think?" I ask when we get to the turquoise L-shaped sectional with a lounge.

Amber bites her lip looking at the price. "It's nice . . .." It is expensive, but not out of my budget.

"I like it." Emily releases my hand and climbs onto the lounge. "It sits good."

"It sits good?"

"Yeah, it sits comfy. Come sit on it, Mommy!"

"Give it a whirl." I nudge Amber and she cuddles next to Emily. I join them, sitting as close as possible to Amber, who tries to scoot away but there is no place for her to go. Wrapping my arm around her shoulders, I pull her into my side. "It does sit comfy."

"You're a goof," Amber mumbles but relaxes a little.

"This goof says we should get it."

"Are you sure?" She cocks her head to the side and peers up at me. All it would take is a little dip of my head and my mouth would be touching hers. Tempting . . . so very tempting.

"It's what you want."

"Are you seriously going to buy this because you know I want it?" Her eyes roam my face.

"Yep."

She rolls her eyes. "You're ridiculous."

"And you're beautiful."

"Can I help you folks?" a sales associate asks with a full watt smile. He's an older gentleman with thinning hair, a potbelly, and a mismatching suit, but he gives off good vibes.

"We're interested in this setup here." I wave at the sectional display we are still sitting on.

"Great, come with me and we will get the paperwork started."

"Shall we?" I stand, holding a hand out to Amber, but she ignores it and picks up Emily, putting her on her hip. Emily is a bit too big to be carried by Amber, and I chuckle at her attempt to keep her distance.

The paperwork doesn't take long and Amber and Emily wander around the store while I finalize the purchase and negotiate delivery.

Luckily, I will be able to have it delivered before Thanksgiving. I want Amber's first Thanksgiving to be perfect, even if the kids won't be there.

When I finish up, I scan for my girls and find them in the kid's furniture section, talking with a young man who is making Emily giggle. I pick up my pace.

"Standing a little close, aren't we?" I growl at the man, molding my hand around Amber's waist and pulling her back into my chest. She lets out a little squeak but doesn't move.

"My apologies. Your daughter was telling me about her pink sparkle room," the man says and takes a step back. I like that he thinks Emily is my daughter.

"Ready to go?" I ask Amber, not bothering to correct the man.

"Yes."

"You folks have a nice day. Come back if you decide you want the bedroom set. I bet it will look great in your room, Emily."

"Sure," I mutter, not liking that he knows Emily's name. I grab Amber's hand, pulling her and Emily away.

"You didn't have to be so rude," Amber whispers as we exit the store.

"How else would he know you are off-limits?" I shrug, watching for cars as we cross the parking lot to my truck.

"He wasn't flirting; he was trying to sell me something."

"He was flirting," I deadpan before I open her door. Picking Emily up, I open the extended cab door and place her on her booster seat.

"Luke, will you be Mommy's boyfriend?" Emily asks as I fasten her seatbelt.

"Yes."

Amber angles around to glare at me. "No."

"Sorry, Emily asked and I answered. You're stuck with me." I laugh and shut Emily's door, then Amber's, cutting off her protests.

When we walk into the empty house, Amber's still explaining to Emily that we are not together, but Emily just giggles.

"It doesn't work that way," Amber huffs, not willing to give it up.

"But Parker's friend Jacob asked me to be Parker's boyfriend and I said yes, and now he's my boyfriend," Emily fires back, getting my attention.

I stop and stare down at Emily. "You are too young for a boyfriend."

"Am not."

"Am too."

"Am not." She puts her little hands on her hips and presses her lips together and squints hard at me. She is just like her mother.

"Amber, help me out here."

"Nope, you're on your own." Amber hangs her coat up and walks to the coffee pot, yawning.

"No boyfriends. Ever," I tell Emily, who rolls her eyes at me. *Rolls her eyes!* She's too young to be rolling her eyes, and much too sweet. "I mean it. No boyfriends."

"Okay." She shrugs off her coat.

"Okay?"

"Yeah, we're getting married at recess." She hangs her coat then walks to Amber. "Can I play on my tablet?"

"Sure," Amber says over her shoulder while adding coffee grounds to the coffee maker.

"Do you even know this Parker character?" I ask, stalking over to Amber. She turns around and leans against the counter with a sly smile. It disappears when I rest my hands on either side of her, pinning her against the counter.

"I . . . I know him," she hesitates, leaning back away from me. "You're too close."

"Not close enough." I press in closer. "But getting there."

"You're not my boyfriend." She sounds breathy and I smile, pressing in closer.

"We don't have to put a label on it."

"That's not what I mean."

"You never say what you mean," I whisper then tentatively brush my lips over hers. She doesn't move but sucks in a breath, and I swoop in. It starts off slow, both reacquainting ourselves, and then her hands slide up my chest and my arms lock around her, pulling her fully into me.

Her tongue mingles with mine and I fist her hair, needing more of her. When she moans, my dick hardens, throbbing against my jeans, and when she wraps her arms around my neck, her tits press up against my chest. I think I might throw caution out the window and have my way with her now instead of taking things slow.

"Making out when little eyes aren't around?" I hear Burns' voice, then the sound of a shutter and a flash goes off. Amber rips her lips away from mine and her face pales.

I don't let Amber go, though she squirms pretty hard.

"What are you doing here, old man?" I growl, glaring at him.

"I tell him he can't just waltz in like he owns the place." Miss Janet smiles at us looking pleased.

"I'm getting good at this photography thing." Burns shows Miss Janet the Polaroid picture. "Putting this on the fridge."

"Let me go." Amber shoves me, sounding distressed.

"Relax." I loosen my grip on her and slide a finger down her cheek then tilt her head up. "To be continued."

She doesn't say anything, which I take as a good sign, but she does take a step away from me, pulling out of my grip.

"We brought over Mrs. Bartley's old barstools. We thought they would look good around your island," Miss Janet says, eyeing the island before she looks at Amber. "Luke, why don't you help Burns bring them in?"

"It's okay, I'll get them," I say, side-eyeing Amber, who hasn't said a word. "I wouldn't want him to break a hip."

"Jackwagon," Burns mutters, setting his Polaroid camera down. "No respect."

# Fight Forever

# 12

## - Amber -

"Are we going to finish what we started, or do you plan to keep yourself as busy as possible so you can avoid me?"

"Son of a biscuit!" I twirl around from where I'm loading the washing machine to find Luke standing at the bottom of the basement stairs. "Don't sneak up on me like that!"

"I had to corner you; otherwise, you'd find some way to avoid me."

"I'm not avoiding you," I lie, turning back toward the washing machine. My cheeks burn just thinking about our kiss earlier. "I've got things to do before I go to work."

"Well, then let me help you." He chuckles. His heavy footsteps clunk against the cement floor, sending my heartrate skyrocketing out of control.

I tried not to replay our moment in the kitchen over and over, but it was mind-blowing. *Wake me up, take my breath away, and leave me wanting more,* mind-blowing. I am so screwed, but a small part of me won't let me give in and get swept away by Luke's charm. There is still a lot of distrust and past wounds I can't ignore.

"You don't need to help. I'm just finishing it up," I say.

"Good, then we can finish what we started," Luke says close to my ear, his breath tickling the side of my face and my legs wobble.

"No," I say on a breath I didn't realize I was holding. Luke's closeness weakens my control over my chaotic, lust-filled emotions. Turning around, I tilt my head up to see Luke's face, the corners of his mouth curves up ever so slightly.

*Stop looking at his mouth!*

"What is holding you back?" Luke asks as his hands gently wrap around my own.

A shiver races down my spine when his thumb gently caresses my knuckles. I bite my lip, looking away from his eyes—eyes that have a way of breaking down my defenses when he looks at me.

"I don't trust you," I blurt out when Luke tilts my head up.

"I know." He swallows. "How do I fix that?"

"I don't know."

"Can we talk about it?" He runs a finger down my temple and tucks a strand of hair behind my ear, and I almost sigh.

"I don't know . . .."

"You're being stubborn again." He chuckles but the smile doesn't reach his eyes. "Come on, I'll make you some coffee."

Luke leads us up the stairs into the mudroom, then releases my hand and walks to the coffee maker while I take a seat on one of the new barstools.

"I don't know where to start," he says over his shoulder.

I look around for the kids. "Maybe this isn't such a good idea . . .."

"Emily and Matt are getting ready for bed. They will be fine," Luke says, taking my coffee cup to the fridge and pouring creamer in it. "I think we need to get this part over with so we can move on to the good stuff."

"You act as if nothing horrible happened between us." I don't want to listen to him brush off the heartbreak he caused all those years ago. It may not have hurt him like it hurt me, but that doesn't give him the right to disregard my feelings. "Do you sweep all your problems under the rug and pretend they don't exist?"

"I'm not trying to sweep anything under the rug; I'm trying to be here for you. Trying to show you that I'm still the man you once loved." Luke sets the coffee cup down in front of me then sits on the barstool and scoots closer. "I didn't want to run off, but at the time, I didn't have much of a choice."

"Why did you run off? You just said it couldn't work and then you were gone. There were so many rumors flying around that I never could figure out what was true and what was a lie."

"I'm not surprised. So many lies were circulating before I left . . . .. I can only imagine they got worse once I was gone." Luke grabs my hand and studies it, lightly tracing the lines across my palm. I want to pull away, but his touch is comforting.

"So, what is the truth?" I finally ask, though it comes out as a whisper.

Luke searches my face for several seconds before he asks, "Do you remember Christine McKnight? Warren's cousin?"

I nod but don't respond.

"There was a party we were both at. Just before you and I started dating. I got pretty wasted and she claims we hooked up. I don't remember any of it. Clint was there and got me home but seven months later, she claimed I had knocked her up."

"I had heard that, but a few months after you left, she married some guy from River Bend."

Luke nods, all emotion has left his face and I don't know how to interpret the look he has now. "Sheriff McKnight Senior told me Christine was pregnant and that I was the father. I denied it. The timing seemed off, too. Clint thought if I had knocked her up, she would be nine months pregnant, but McKnight wasn't going to listen to me over his niece."

"So, you left?" Luke flinches at my tone and I feel a ping of guilt. I know him telling me this is hard, but it was hard picking up the pieces after he left, too. It was hard figuring out what my new future was going to look like. It's hard to feel bad for him when he was the one who broke us.

"Not exactly. I told McKnight that I wanted a paternity test, and he got pissed I would even dare question Christine's word. Not long after, he threw my dad in jail for drunk and disorderly. It wasn't Dad's first time, but McKnight cornered me and said that if I didn't step up and take responsibility for Christine and the baby, he would slap an assaulting an officer charge on my dad. He'd be behind bars for years and my brothers would be put into foster care because there was no way McKnight would let me be their guardian."

"Did your dad really assault an officer?" I ask, absently touching his forearm. Luke glances down to where my hand is and looks relieved. I want to pull it away, but I can't seem to muster that kind of meanness. Luke's dad was always a source of pain for him.

"I'll never know for sure. My dad was a mean bastard. I wouldn't have put it past him . . .." Luke sucks in a deep breath then tilts my head so he can search my eyes. "I wanted to tell you everything, but I was young and naïve and didn't want it to get out and jeopardize my brothers. I didn't care if my dad was sent to jail, but I cared about what would happen to them. You knew how Jax was back then. How all of them were. Clint would have gotten out of the system unscathed, but Eric and Jax would have landed in juvie and don't think McKnight didn't threaten to have them locked up.

"So, I told McKnight I would join the military and get set up so I could take care of Christine and the baby. It was the last thing I wanted to do, but I didn't have much of a choice. He put me in a spot where I had to choose you or my brothers. I didn't even know if you would want me if you knew Christine was pregnant, so I did what I thought was best and ended things with you. I should have told you the truth about it all, but I couldn't. I didn't want to end things with you but mostly, I didn't want to see you disappointed in me."

"Oh." I'm not sure how to process that information. Luke had to step up for his brothers when his dad decided to stop being a parent. I'm not surprised he put them first, but a baby? He's never once mentioned having a kid. "So, you have a kid?"

"No." He frowns and shakes his head. I shouldn't feel relieved but I am. I knew Luke wasn't exactly a saint when it came to girls back in high school. I made him prove to me he wasn't after me for just sex before I agreed to go on a date with him. A lot of what he is telling me does make me feel a little bit better about him leaving, but it still doesn't change the fact that he did. If I have learned anything, it's that men can change their minds without thinking about the damage it does to others. "I lied and told McKnight in order for Christine and the baby to get on my military insurance a paternity test had to be done, and surprise, surprise . . . it wasn't my baby."

"Wow." I sigh then duck my head so he can't read my thoughts. To see the truth still doesn't fully fix the pain. He could have come back after that, but still, he waited fifteen years. Why now? And what if he decides to leave again? What if living here with me and the kids isn't what he thought it was going to be and wants out?

"Hey, look at me. What are you thinking?" He tries to tilt my chin, but I dodge it.

"I'm glad things worked out for you," I mumble, still ducking my head. I don't easily cry; I've grown a thick skin over these last fifteen years, but I want to cry now. None of what he's told me makes me trust him. If anything, I worry that he'll bolt if things go bad.

"Worked out for me?" he scoffs. "Everything that happened to me was out of my control."

"I know, I get it. So, you left and waited fifteen years to come back." I nod and attempt a sympathetic smile. I really don't want to cry but my nose stings and if I sit here much longer, I know I will.

"I didn't wait fifteen years to come back. I came the second I was able. I came back for you, Amber," Luke says, the laughter in his eyes is gone, replaced with anguish.

My head snaps up. "When?"

"I wanted as much distance between McKnight and Christine as possible, so I signed up for anything that would keep me away. Tours or training. Anything. By the time I found out the truth, I was committed. It was two years after we broke up that I was able to get leave to come back. You weren't home. You were visiting Henry's family for the holidays."

"Oh."

"Yeah . . . oh."

We sit in silence for several seconds until Luke slides a hand around the side of my neck and stands from the barstool. I peer up at him wishing I could trust him fully but not ready to.

"What are you thinking?" he asks, searching my face for a sign of forgiveness.

"I understand why you left, Luke, I do, but I still don't trust you. Not fully."

"Then I'm just going to have to change your mind."

# 13

## - Luke -

Two days since I told Amber everything and our seemingly opposite schedules have kept us apart. Not exactly helping me prove that she can trust me, but I have a plan. One that will prove she can trust me again, but first, I need to kiss her like she has never been kissed before. It's the first stage of my plan, so I wait until she finishes putting the kids to bed to start *Operation Kiss Amber Senseless.*

"Amber?" I call from the bedroom door and she opens her bathroom door holding a toothbrush in her mouth, still wearing her scrubs.

She has to leave for work soon, but not before I get my fix.

I made sure to take my shirt off before kick-starting this little plan of mine. I've seen the way she stares at me when I'm shirtless, and I'm rewarded with a lust-eyed pursual.

"I need toothpaste." I don't, but she doesn't know that. She opens the bathroom door wider and turns to finish brushing her teeth. I take that as permission to enter.

"Help yourself," she says around her toothbrush, looking at my abs through the mirror. *Don't mind if I do.*

She quickly finishes brushing her teeth then ties her hair up in a ponytail while I lean against the doorframe and watch.

"Did you want to take it?" She turns to look at me over her shoulder.

"No, I'm good."

"Why are you looking at me like that?" Looking nervous, she fidgets with her hair, and I flash her a hungry smile.

"Just admiring the view."

"I've got to get to work." She rolls her eyes and her cheeks pinken.

"How much time do you have before you need to leave?" I ask, stepping from the doorframe to stand directly behind her.

"Why?"

I don't answer. Instead, I put a hand on her hip and dip my head to kiss her neck. My dick grows hard and she lets out a tiny gasp when I pull her back so she can feel exactly what she does to me.

"When do I get to take you out?" I whisper against the shell of her ear. "Or get some alone time with you?"

"I . . . don't know," she says then sucks in a tiny breath when my hand slides around her ribs, my thumb lightly caressing the underside of her bra. "I have to go to work."

"Not until I get some of your attention."

"What kind of attention?"

"I want your mouth." I turn her so quickly, she stumbles into my chest, right where I want her, and I slam my mouth against hers. Her lip gloss tastes like cherries mixed with the mint of her toothpaste, and I wouldn't normally like the taste if it wasn't mingled with Amber's own distinct flavor.

Her fingers slide through my hair—it's the first time she's really let herself kiss me back and it's fucking fantastic. I take more of her because I know I can't have her for much longer. She whimpers and I am so screwed. I don't think I'm strong enough to let her go, but I have to be. I need to take baby steps with Amber, not giant leaps.

My hand slides down her scrub pants and I grab her ass. All I want to do is haul her over my shoulder and throw her onto the bed so I can worship every inch of her; but instead, I mentally tell myself I need to slow it down. I also mentally curse myself, and reluctantly, I pull back and groan when I see her eyes flutter open, filled with desire for more.

"Damn, I wish you didn't have to work."

"That was cruel." She lays her head against my chest. "I can't work with sick people if that kiss keeps playing on repeat."

I chuckle and kiss the top of her head. "I want you all to myself. Soon."

She smiles up at me then steps from my embrace. "Maybe . . .."

"What do you mean, maybe?" I slit my eyes at her.

She sighs, side-stepping me. "Luke, I have so much to do before Thanksgiving. Can we talk about this later?"

"I'll cancel Thanksgiving," I warn at her turned back.

"You won't," she hollers over her shoulder and walks out of the bathroom.

*Well fuck. That didn't go according to plan.*

\*\*\*\*\*

"Your couch is teal," Burns notes as he walks through the front door without knocking.

"You can't just storm into Luke and Amber's home without knocking, Burns. It's rude," Miss Janet reprimands and for good measure, knocks him upside the head.

"Wish I had my camera for that," I mutter as I get up from the couch and greet the old man and his new wife.

"These boys used to run through my place without knocking or being invited! It's my turn to return the favor," Burns quips but Miss Janet ignores him. She gives me a quick peck on the cheek and a nod to Benny before she heads into the kitchen to help Dawn and Amber with the cooking. With Dawn overseeing the Thanksgiving dinner, it will, no doubt, be the most delicious meal imageable.

Amber's mother Linda and Sarah are at the island enjoying some wine and as far as I can tell, getting tipsy and not helping.

"Grab a beer and come watch the game before you put the women in a tizzy, Burns." Benny, Amber's father, points to a cooler we are using as a second coffee table.

"No beer fridge, but you have a teal couch?"

"I thought about it, but then I would have to clean out the garage and walk to the garage. A cooler is more convenient. Thanks for coming."

"Of course, I came. Why wouldn't I? Dawn's cooking." Burns gives me a perplexed look. "Where are my other boys?"

"Jax and Clint went to the store for something Dawn needed, they'll be back soon; and Eric isn't coming."

"That's a shocker. Did he know Sarah was going to be here?" Burns asks, grabbing a beer from the cooler and wiggling his eyebrows toward Sarah.

Benny grabs Burns' beer, grumbling something under his breath, and twists the cap off. "Here, old man."

"I could have done it, and who you callin' old? You're just as old as I am."

"I'm a good twenty years younger," Benny says, slouching back into the seat. "And don't pester Sarah about Eric. Those two need to figure their shit out on their own, just like Amber and Luke are."

"Well, don't treat me like I'm old as dirt," Burns growls and takes a seat next to Benny. "I'm a newlywed."

"You are old as dirt!"

"Older than dirt," I add with a chuckle.

"Watch it, ya jackwagon, or I'll tell Amber to steer clear of ya." Burns glares at me.

"You'll tell me what?" Amber asks as she comes into the living room with the other ladies.

Burns smirks at me. "Your boyfriend is a jackwagon."

"What else is new?" Amber leans over the couch to kiss Burns' cheek. "And he isn't my boyfriend."

"We aren't labeling us quite yet." That gets me an eye roll.

"There's nothing to label."

"Only a matter of time," I murmur as she heads back toward the kitchen and yes, I scan her backside. She has a great ass—and I haven't been able to keep my hands off it lately. She may not consider me her boyfriend yet, but she's letting me get a few stolen kisses.

"I'm rooting for you," Sarah says to me softly before she heads over to greet Burns. "Hello, Burns, it's always a pleasure to see you."

"Don't be so hoity-toity around me, Sarah. I like you better when you let your spunk out." Burns pats her back while she hugs him.

"You are in a mood today." Dawn smiles, moving in for her hug.

How the hell does the grumpy bastard get all the women to swoon over him?

"Sweetness, it smells delicious in here. You have my mouth watering." Burns hugs her a little longer. Too bad Clint isn't here to witness the old man and his flirtatious ways. "When's the bird going to be done?"

"In about an hour. We made a ton of food, so I hope you're hungry."

"I wore my expandable pants," he says proudly, demonstrating the elasticity of his pants.

Leaving us men to our football game, the women head back into the kitchen. Burns takes a seat and looks around. "Where are the kids?"

"They're with Henry," I grumble. I've hated not having the kids around, even if it has been only one day. I've grown used to their presence and it feels empty without them here.

"What was Eric's excuse for not coming?"

"There is reward money for information or the capture of Dawn's ex, and Eric thinks he has the best shot at bringing him in," I share, then look over at Benny for more details.

He furrows his brow. "What are you looking at me for?"

"Sarah's been working with the FBI to make sure Dawn's whereabouts don't show up in any of their reports."

"Okay?" He continues to eye me with a frown.

"The boy's trying to ask if they are working together," Burns says over his beer bottle.

"How the hell would I know?" Benny quips.

"She's your daughter," I offer with a shrug.

"He's your brother," Benny shoots back.

"Eric doesn't tell me shit." I sigh, taking a swig from my beer. "I didn't even know Sarah and Eric were a thing."

Benny shrugs. "It was a long time ago while you were in the service."

Time for another part of my plan, *Operation Get Amber's Family Onboard*. I always got the feeling

Benny and Linda liked me, but they probably heard some of the unflattering rumors Christine was pushing all those years ago. Not to mention Amber's reluctance may give them reservations.

"About me and Amber . . ." I say, then clear my throat. "Is that going to be a problem with you and Linda?"

"Sounds like you and Amber aren't a thing," Burns comments with a smug grin on his wrinkled face.

"*If* it happens. Linda and I are thrilled; we always liked you. I don't know what happened all those years ago, but if Amber forgave you, then I don't see the need to dwell on the past, either," Benny says, extending his beer bottle and I tap it with my own. Not exactly what I was hoping for, but I'll take it. Linda and Sarah will be my stronger allies anyway.

"Thanks, Benny, I appreciate that."

The front door swings open, tearing my attention from Benny to see Eric standing in the doorway. "Jesus, I forgot how cold it gets up here."

"What the hell are you doing here?" Shocked to see Eric, I don't immediately stand from the couch.

"What the hell are you doing here?" Sarah says from where she sits at the kitchen island.

"What? I can't visit my brothers on Thanksgiving?" Eric asks, dropping his bag and apparently, unconcerned with my heating bill, doesn't shut the door right away.

"Can you shut the door?" I wave at my younger brother, who wasn't born in a barn—I should know because I taught him better.

Burns stands and points to his wife. "I told you I should have brought my camera!"

"Shut it, Burns," Eric and Sarah say at the same time.

Thanksgiving is going to be fun.

# Fight Forever

# 14

## - Amber -

"They didn't have any fresh pineapple, but they had the pre-cut stuff. It says fresh on it," Clint says as he comes through the back door into the kitchen and sets two grocery bags onto the island.

"What the hell did we miss?" Jax asks, following Clint with a case of beer.

"Eric decided to make a surprise appearance," Sarah says looking a little shellshocked. "I'm going to need more wine."

"Nice seeing you, too!" Eric hollers at her back, flashing a cocky grin that looks eerily similar to Luke's.

"Are we pretending that nothing just happened in there?" Dawn asks Sarah quietly, pointing the knife she's using to cut potatoes at Eric. "Like we're pretending Luke and Amber aren't a thing?"

"I think I liked it better when you didn't talk much," Sarah muttered before gulping the rest of her wine.

"You insisted I break out of my shell and now you're complaining?" Dawn smiles and rolls her eyes.

"What happened between you two? You seemed fine at Burns and Janet's wedding?" I ask, glancing over my shoulder, watching Luke and his brothers reunite.

"I'll tell you as soon as you tell us what's going on between you and Luke. As your lawyer, I need to know the details." Sarah returns, pouring a large amount of wine into her glass, sparing only the briefest of glances toward Eric.

"We're exploring . . .? I'm not sure I want to call him my boyfriend yet." I lift my shoulders. "Yeah, he told Emily he'd be my boyfriend, but he didn't ask me. He just makes decisions about us and leaves me out of it, and when I call him out on it, he just kisses me until I shut up."

"So . . . you are together?" Janet asks, looking confused.

"No . . . I mean, yes if you ask Luke, but no if you ask me."

"I'm not following. Is this how women play hard to get now?" my mom asks and Janet giggles.

"I'm not playing hard to get," I groan. "I just think he should talk to me before making assumptions about our relationship."

"You're being stubborn," my mother scoffs, giving me her signature pointed stare. "Sounds like you are together."

"Whatever. Can we please move on to what is happening between Sarah and Eric?"

"Fine," Sarah groans. "Eric just learned I helped work a deal with Dawn's ex, Darin."

Dawn stops cutting the potatoes to look at Sarah in shock but doesn't say anything. "He's willing to testify against the Port Pirates in return for protective custody through the trial and protective relocation after the trial. That's really all I can say on the matter," Sarah explains.

Dawn's ex is the reason she went on the run a few months ago to escape his motorcycle club. I don't know all the details, but I know they managed to find her, and it brought her ex out of hiding and now he's on the run.

Visibly pale over the news, Dawn whispers, "Why didn't you tell me?"

"I was . . . after Thanksgiving. I didn't want Clint going all caveman, and I didn't want you to worry. I wanted you to enjoy a family get together," Sarah confesses, and she looks a little guilty over not telling Dawn sooner. "I had to tell Eric to stop looking for Darin so the FBI could bring him in safely. Eric was pissed that I was even in contact with Darin and didn't tell him. We didn't exactly end the conversation on friendly terms."

"Why didn't you tell him you were talking to Darin?" Dawn asks as Janet takes the knife from her and continues to chop the potatoes.

"Darin reached out to me, said if you trusted me then so could he, and he wanted to know if I would help him. I didn't want anyone to know I was in contact with him until I spoke to the agent conducting the investigation on the Port Pirates."

"So, what does this all mean?" I ask, keeping an eye on Dawn, who takes a seat, worry marring her face as she rubs her pregnant belly.

"It means Dawn will be safe from her past very soon." Sarah smiles and leans over to put a hand over Dawn's. "This is good news; stop worrying. Just be a little patient and don't do anything stupid that will bring attention to you. Before you know it, all the bad shit that went down back in Charleston will be behind you."

"Define anything stupid?" Dawn whispers, not sounding at all reassured.

Sarah eyes her suspiciously. "Why?"

"Clint thinks I should start a cooking blog," she confesses and looks around at us all. "Where I share my mother's recipes and offer cooking advice."

"That's a brilliant idea!" Janet says while sliding the cut potatoes into a pot of water. "I'd absolutely follow you, even if I am technology inept."

Dawn hesitates. "He thinks I should call it *Colson Cooking*."

"I think that's a great idea," Sarah says and squeezes her hand. "Maybe not share your picture online, though."

"You think I should do it?"

"I love the idea," I chime in with a smile, happy to see my friend finally starting to live her life.

"Now, can we talk about you and Luke?" Sarah asks looking exasperated. "He came back hotter than he left, and it has been way too long since you've been with a man. Why not give things a shot?"

Looking over at Luke, I can't deny he is more than a lot hotter than he was fifteen years ago. "I'm not sure I can trust him," I say, looking away from him. "I know we live together . . . but what if more drama complicates things? Or we fizzle out? I would be back living with my parents, and Henry would have more ammunition to fire at me."

"Luke and you never had to worry about fizzling out. You and Henry may have fizzled out, but that's just because you two never should have been together in the first place. And playing the 'what if' game leads to a road to loneliness. I think you need to grab on to Luke and the happiness he brings you and the kids and hold on tight," my mom says, getting agreement from the rest of the women.

"I think I need to take it a bit slow and not just grab on tight." I roll my eyes but the idea of letting go of my fear feels refreshing. I want to trust Luke, really trust him, but there is a piece of me that is scared, even if being with Luke has felt like stepping out of a cave and into a sunny day. The kind of sunny day you wish the sun didn't have to set.

"You told me to grab onto Clint and look at me now. I'm having a baby and about to get married, *and* I guess I'm starting a cooking blog," Dawn says, standing from her chair to check on the potatoes Janet is hovering over.

"I'm pretty sure that was Sarah who told you to grab on, and if Luke puts a baby in me without asking first like Clint did, I might kill him."

"So, you two *have* had sex." Sarah winks at me with a teasing smile.

"No, we haven't had sex." I move around the island and grab the wine. "I'm cutting you off."

"No!"

"Why don't you want Luke's babies?" my mom asks, trying to sound nonchalant, but I know she wants more grandbabies in her life.

"I'm not saying I don't want his babies . . . I just know the Colson men. When they want something, they don't tend to ask. They like making the decisions and telling you about it later . . .. No offense, Dawn."

"None taken. I'm happy, and if Clint hadn't taken our future into his own hands, I might be off the grid living a miserable existence in another small town."

"Or dead," Sarah adds.

"True."

"This went dark fast. Let's go back to babies and when I will get me some more grandbabies." Mom looks at me, hopeful and giddy.

"Mom, stop!" I cry out. "I'm not having Luke's babies anytime soon."

"But you will have my babies?" Luke's voice rumbles from the edge of the kitchen.

Janet and my mom burst out into laughter as I slowly swivel around to face Luke, hoping the heat climbing up my neck won't flush my cheeks with embarrassment.

Luke comes closer, grabbing a cherry tomato from the vegetable tray on the island, looking like he hit the jackpot.

"We should start practicing now," he says softly, but not soft enough that the others can't hear. Sex with Luke would be nice, even if I'm not ready to fully trust him. The way he always finds a way to touch me has been a constant turn on, waking parts of me that I thought were dormant. For several days now I've wanted him to take things to the next level and see if we are just as explosive as we were when we were teenagers.

"You should wait at least thirty minutes after you eat," Janet adds, and she and my mom start laughing harder.

"Noted." He winks at me, popping the cherry tomato into his mouth, a silent promise in his eyes that excites me.

*****

"I thought they would never leave," Luke mutters as we wave goodbye to everyone and shuts the door.

"Where am I crashing?" Eric asks, lifting his bag over his shoulder.

"You can take Matt's room," I tell Eric.

"I've got some work I need to get done. I'll see you guys in the morning. Night," Eric says over his shoulder and climbs the stairs.

"Today was fun." Luke raises his eyebrows with a mischievous smile and tingles shoot down to my core. I know exactly what is on his mind.

"Today was exhausting." I sigh and turn away, but Luke grabs my arm, spinning me around and pulling me into his chest. Have I mentioned how nice his chest is?

His mouth captures mine, and I give into the kiss immediately like I have all week. I melt into him when his tongue thrusts its way into my mouth. More tingles shoot through me and my body hums with anticipation.

A week of little tastes and playful teasing and I'm a hot, writhing addict. I press in as close as I can get and he rips his mouth from mine, leaving me unsatisfied.

"Want to talk about those babies?" he asks with a taunting smile that makes me bite my lip.

I roll my eyes. "I think you took that way out of context."

"So, you ladies weren't talking about us having babies?" he asks, running a hand down my spine. I want to purr like a cat.

"You don't plan to let that go, do you?"

"Nope."

"You need to stop touching me like that . . . unless you plan to make a move," I say with a coy smile.

"Oh, I'll make a move . . .." His hand goes up the back of my shirt and I whimper a little. "But you've been stubborn, so I think I'll wait until you beg for it."

"Nope." I shake my head, biting back a smile and attempt to step away from his hold but he only tugs me closer, tightening his hold on me.

"So stubborn," he hisses through a clenched jaw. His hands wander down to my ass and he hoists me up. I squeak and cling to his shoulders as my legs wrap around his waist, and we are already on the move down the hallway to our rooms.

He toes open my bedroom door and walks to the bed, laying me down on my back before pinning me with his weight.

Hovering over me, his nose caresses my neck, ear, and cheek before he kisses me tenderly. I can feel him hard against my core, but it isn't good enough, and I almost beg.

"When do I get that full-course meal?" he asks, kissing down my neck.

I smile and lift my hips to press harder against his erection. "When you beg for more than just an appetizer."

He cups my breast over my shirt and I can see him contemplate his next move. My nipples grow hard when his thumb skims over them. I nibble his ear and he groans. I have him right where I want him.

For two weeks, Luke has had the upper hand—using my body against me, pushing us to this moment—and I know it's going to be great, but I like having a little bit of dominance over him.

Slipping my hands under his shirt, I feel nothing but hard muscles and smooth skin. I have the urge to taste every inch of Luke's body as I push his shirt farther up.

"What are you doing?" He watches me push up his shirt more.

"I want to feel you, skin to skin," I say, looking away from his muscled abdomen to his eyes, which are fully dilated and hungry with desire.

He grips me tight, then seeks out my mouth with his, crushing me to him, his desperate movements are a testimony to his failing restraint. Pulling my hair gently to get access to my neck, he kisses down and up again, nipping at my ear. His hands find their way under my shirt, and he breaks our connection long enough to pull it over my head.

Sitting back on his heels, Luke stares down at me with so much admiration that it warms my heart.

"I've dreamed of this moment since I first returned to Peak Valley."

Looking up at him, he looks vulnerable and it only makes me more confident. Luke is never vulnerable, and I love that he will be with me and is not afraid to lose control.

"What are you waiting for?"

Luke grabs my wrists and pulls me up and off the bed to stand before him.

Luke's hands are on my hips, pulling me to him, kissing me hard with desperate need. I tug on the hem of his shirt, needing to feel his skin against my own. Luke reaches behind his head and pulls off his shirt. It's the sexiest thing I've seen in years . . . until I see his perfectly chiseled pecs and washboard abs. Tentatively, I touch his stomach, feeling the hard planes and smooth warm skin. Moving up to his chest, I fight the urge to lick him. I make the mistake of looking up at him and his hungry grin.

"My turn," he says, reaching for my hip, hoisting me up, and carrying me back to the bed. I attack his pants, not holding back. My need for him is so great, and again, I almost beg.

"Hurry," I demand while unhooking my bra and ripping it from me.

"Fuck," he hisses, his eyes now a torrent of emotion. His jaw clenches as he stares down at my completely naked body.

"Take your clothes off," I order. "I want to see you."

Slowly, painfully slow, he pushes his jeans and boxer briefs down. His dick is hard and long and is pointing at me like it knows where it belongs.

Licking my lips, I like what I see. I want to taste him the way I know he wants to taste me.

"You keep looking at me like that and this will be over quicker than I want," Luke says, putting a knee on the bed and crawling on top of me. "I want to take my time; I've wanted you for too fucking long."

His fingers trace up my stomach and my body hums with anticipation. Palming one breast, Luke's warm lips seek out the other. My head thrashes back as he licks around my hardened nipple. His mouth releases my breast, then trails kisses down my stomach until he reaches my pussy and stops. A finger slowly glides through my folds, and I arch my hips for more, but he only watches through his thick lashes. There's a smile that plays across his face, and I can't stop the whimper that escapes. "Luke, please." I grip the blanket.

"Beg again." His finger glides through my folds again, stopping on my clit.

"*Please.*"

His head drops and his tongue touches my clit, causing me to buck hard. He puts a hand on my stomach, holding me down, and spreads my legs wider before he licks, sucks, and eats me out as if he can never get full. I don't want him to stop, I want him to feast on me from now until eternity. He slides a finger inside me and there is no warning, no build up . . . just an explosion of sensation as I come hard. My body convulses and Luke keeps licking and sucking until I whimper his name. A shiver runs up and down the length of my body as he lifts his head and kisses my inner thigh. I think I might be dreaming; I'm in a daze.

"Amber?" He kisses my stomach, and I hum in response. "Do I need a condom?"

"Hmm?" I can't really focus on words, just the sensations his kisses are causing.

"Condom?" he asks and hovers over me. I don't really register his words, but I want to feel him, now, inside me. "I have to go to my room and get one."

Did he say go? "You have to go?"

"I'll be back. I have to get a condom." He moves to lift from the bed and my legs wind tightly around him. I don't want him to go.

"Amber?"

"I'm on birth control," I blurt out and his face softens.

"You sure?" He nudges my entrance.

"Yes."

Luke thrusts once and I'm full, so full I can't stop the whimper that escapes my lips. My legs squeeze tighter around him, pulling him in more. I want him to go deeper.

"God, you're tight. So tight. I need a minute." Luke sucks in a breath.

"Luke, I need you to move. Now." I circle my hips and he slams his mouth against mine, muffling his groan. He pulls out and I moan down his throat. I want him back inside me. He drives in hard, and it jolts me back.

Ripping my mouth from his, I cry out with pleasure I've never felt before, not like this. Grabbing his biceps, I meet him thrust for thrust. Circling my hips, he hits all the right spots.

My muscles tense as the pressure deep in my lower belly builds. This time I'm not surprised when I start to come. I savor it, letting it build more and more until I'm so high, I crash hard, screaming Luke's name.

Luke kisses me hard, pounding harder and faster until he rips his mouth from mine, pulling me tight against his chest, and releasing deep inside me.

Slowly we come back down from the most euphoric high I have ever had. I don't want Luke to let me go, I need him to hold me together. There's no going back after this.

Luke rolls to his side, pulling me with him and tucking me into his side.

"I think you broke me," Luke murmurs into my hair.

"We were always good at that . . . but I don't remember it being that good." I sigh as I throw my leg over his thigh.

"Next time will be even better."

"I don't know . . . that might be hard to top," I tease, tracing the ridges of his abs.

"I made you beg." Luke kisses me with a smile and I mentally think of a few ways to make him beg next time.

# Fight Forever

# 15

## - Luke -

"This place is a mess," Burns says from the entrance of my garage. "Am I first to get here?"

"Burns? That you?" I call from deep inside the garage where I'm looking for Christmas lights. I know they've got to be somewhere around here.

With Christmas only a few weeks away, I need to get started on hanging the lights and getting a tree for Matt and Emily to decorate. I want their Christmas here in this house to be special. A kind of Christmas they will never forget.

"Of course, it's me. Who else would it be?"

"Clint, Benny, Eric, or Jax?" I retort, picking up a box that is covered in layers of dust.

"Am I the first to get here?"

"Yeah," I breathe out, carrying the box through the maze of crap I keep stored in the garage. I need to clean it out, but I've been so focused on finishing the house and finding new ways to make Amber beg for me, I've been a bit preoccupied.

"Damn, I was hoping I'd get here when Dawn arrived."

"She's about to be a married woman and last I checked, you were a newlywed yourself," I tease, wiping off some of the dust before opening the box.

"Jackwagon thinks he's funny," Burns grumbles under his breath. "Clint texted. Dawn is bringing over some chili. I'm starving."

"I thought you were coming here to help hang Christmas lights."

"I'm supervising, but not until I get some of Dawn's chili." Burns chuckles, finding an old lawn chair and sits. "Are you planning to burn the house down?"

"Not funny, old man," I growl as I pull out knotted strings of Christmas lights. "I should get some new ones."

"Call Jax and have him bring over the extra he bought for Janet's house." Burns waves me off. "Who do you know that drives a Jaguar?"

"That would be Henry," I grumble, throwing the old Christmas lights back into their box and emerge from the garage.

Emily and Matt jump out of the car, not sparing a glance my way, and I'm instantly on alert.

"Hey, kiddos." I wave at them.

Matt briefly glances my way then looks at Henry, who is climbing out of his car. Henry says something to the kids that visibly upsets Matt and confuses Emily, though I can't hear what it is. With a curt nod, Matt takes Emily's hand and leads her to the house.

Henry comes around the front of the car. "We need to have a chat."

"Not sure there is anything we need to say to each other," I reply.

"Need me to cover your back?" Burns whispers at my side.

"No, I think I can handle this. Go in and make sure the kids are okay."

"I'll make this quick." Henry rocks back on his heels with a shit-eating grin. "I think it's best if you stopped playing house with Amber."

"Playing house?" I ask, crossing my arms. "And if I don't?"

"Things will get difficult for Amber."

"Is that a threat?"

"I don't make threats; I'm not a hoodlum like you." Henry points a finger at me like that's supposed to get his message across. "I did my research on you, Luke. You and your brothers are nothing but trouble, and I won't have that around my children."

Unable to stop the laugh that bubbles up, I shake my head. Henry lowers his hand, pursing his lips. I'm not buying his bullshit. None of my brothers have been in any kind of trouble. We may have been rowdy when we were kids but nothing got us thrown into jail or caused anyone to get hurt.

"You're full of shit. You know how I know you're full of shit?" I take a step closer to Henry, who fumbles back half a step, clearly not expecting me to stand up for Amber, which pisses me off more. "You have to use amateur scare tactics to try to get me to back off, but I got news for you, Henry . . . .. I'm not scared of you and neither is Amber. And for the record, I'm not going anywhere."

"You have no idea who you're messing with," Henry says with a shakiness in his tone that only makes me bark with laughter.

"I think you better leave before you embarrass yourself some more," I snarl, stepping closer to him. His eyes widen when I lean in, clear my throat, then spit down at his feet.

"She's going to lose those kids!" Henry cries out, but I've already turned away from him and continue to head for the house.

"We'll see about that," I holler over my shoulder before taking the steps up the porch where Burns is recording the whole exchange.

"If I knew how to put this on YouTube, I would." Burns chuckles. "I swear the man was so scared of you, he nearly pissed his pants."

"Give me that." I snatch his phone and replay the video for a few seconds before I send a copy of it to my cell. "You won't be sharing that with anyone."

"I know, you jackwagon." Burns takes his phone back and blocks me from going into the house. "I figured what was being said needed to be recorded. The man rubs me the wrong way."

"That makes two of us." I run a hand down my face, turning to watch Henry back too quickly out of the driveway. He's up to something. I can feel it.

"Those kids are upset. You need to calm down before you go in there, then love on them, because whatever happened at their father's tore them up. They have that sad look in their eye like you and your brothers use to get when your dad got mean-drunk."

"You think he hurt them?" I try to sidestep Burns, but the old man can be quick when he wants to be.

"No, not physically . . . at least from what I can tell, but he hurt their hearts for sure. Go in there and love on them. I'll call Jax and have him bring over the extra Christmas lights when he brings Janet over. A little decorating should help cheer them up."

"Thanks, Burns."

"Go." He pats my shoulder and finally moves out of the way.

When I get inside, the kids aren't in the living room. I rush up the stairs, taking two at a time, trying to stay quiet and not wake Amber, who is working her last night shift tonight.

Glancing in Emily's room, I find it's empty, so I move to Matt's room and knock quietly on the door before entering. "How are my favorite little humans?"

"Luke!" Emily jumps from Matt's bed and then stops and looks back at her brother.

Stepping farther inside, I scoop her up and carry her over to Matt's bed and sit next to him. "Everything okay?"

Matt shrugs but doesn't look at me while Emily lays her head on my chest and frowns. "Do you want to talk about it?"

Emily looks up at me and her head almost knocks into my chin. Big tears form in her eyes and she whispers, "Why are you leaving, Luke?"

"I'm not leaving."

"Daddy said you had to leave because you are a bad man, but I told him not all giants were bad," Emily rambles, clutching me in a tight hug. "Right, Luke? You're a good giant, right?"

Pure rage turns my vision red and I want to rip Henry's head off. Sucking in a deep breath and pushing my anger aside, I hug Emily and hope they don't pick up on the underlining anger I have in my tone. "I'm a good giant, Emily. I think you're right. I think your dad doesn't know that some giants are good."

"See, Matt, I was right," Emily squeals in my lap. "And you're not leaving?"

"I'm not leaving." I kiss the top of her head then pick her up off my lap and set her down on her feet. "Why don't you go change into some clothes you can get dirty, and dress warm. We're going to hang some Christmas lights on the house when my brother Jax gets here. Eric is getting a tree to put in the living room, too."

"Yay!" Emily jumps up and down with her fists in the air. "I want to put the star on top."

"Okay, now go on so I can talk with your brother," I say.

"Okay!"

"Are we okay?" I ask Matt, who side-eyes me.

Looking down at his feet, Matt mumbles, "My dad said we have to live with him."

"Do you want to live with your dad?"

Matt looks up at me perplexed, like he wasn't aware he had a choice before he looks back at his feet and shakes his head no.

"You should talk to your mom and let her know you don't want to live with him."

Matt nods, looking like the weight of the world is on his shoulders. I would give anything to take that weight and carry it myself.

"I'm sorry you are in this position. It isn't fair." I sigh, rubbing his back. "If I could change things, I would."

"Thanks, Luke," Matt murmurs then surprises the heck out of me and hugs me. Well damn, if that didn't feel good.

"One more thing I wanted to talk to you about . . .." I clear my throat and Matt looks at me with a slight frown. "I should have talked to you sooner, but I wanted to ask you how you felt about me dating your mom."

"Dating my mom? You mean being her boyfriend?" Matt squints at me. Maybe he's too young for this conversation, but it occurred to me that I should make sure Matt doesn't feel like I'm coming in and taking over as the man of the house when he's carried the title for some time now.

"Yeah, you okay with me being your mom's boyfriend?"

"Yeah, I guess so." He shrugs and bounces his leg nervously.

"Your mom will always put you and Emily first, so I don't want either of you to think I'm taking her away from you."

"I don't think that." Matt shakes his head. "We like having you around. And your brothers."

"Good, I like being around." I ruffle his hair. "And I'm not going anywhere unless it is what your mom wants."

"Okay."

"Are you hungry, or have you and Emily eaten?"

"We haven't eaten."

"Good, because Dawn is bringing over some chili soon, and then my brothers and I will hang the Christmas lights up on the house. You want to help us?"

"Yes! Can I get on the roof?"

"Um, maybe? We need to talk to your mom about that, but she needs her sleep, so let's wait and ask a little later." I chuckle remembering how adventurous Jax used to be, climbing to places that should be out of reach for him when he was Matt's age. Hopefully, Matt won't grow up to be as reckless as Jax. "Alright, let's go find Burns and make sure he doesn't eat all the chili the second Dawn arrives."

*****

"You jackwagons aren't doing it right. You don't staple the lights; you put hooks up," Burns yells from his lawn chair in the middle of the lawn, critiquing our every move. "Tell 'em, Emily."

"You're doing it wrong, you jackwagons!"

"Whoa!" I look over my shoulder as Benny smacks the back of Burns' head.

"Watch your pie hole in front of my granddaughter," Benny chastises and Emily giggles.

"Emily, we don't say jackwagon," Amber says from the porch where she's snuggled under blankets with Linda, Dawn, and Miss Janet, drinking hot chocolate and listening to Christmas music to help us 'stay in the Christmas spirit' while we work, and they watch.

"Okay, Mommy." Emily giggles when Burns ruffles her hair and winks at her. I don't think I want to know what the old man is teaching her. Better to let Benny handle that situation.

Emily seems to have bounced back to her cheerful self since returning from her father's, but Matt is still a little quiet and distant. Matt and Jax have been laying out the strands of lights and checking to make sure they work. A few times I've heard him laugh at something Jax said, but I'm still worried about him.

I need to tell Amber what happened, but she only just woke up and is having a good time with the women. I just don't want to ruin it. She's been less stressed over the whole Henry situation since his last confrontation, and this would only bring it front and center again.

"Dawn mentioned is having a small bachelorette party," Clint says from the bottom of the ladder I'm on.

"Really? So, does that mean you want a bachelor party now?"

"No, but Dawn says I have to get you out of the house for theirs."

"I can do that," I say, stapling a strand of lights up.

"I'll order the stripper," Jax chimes in and then looks over to Matt. "Don't tell your mom."

"Make him pay for your silence," Eric says as he walks past them with a second ladder.

Matt holds out his hand with a smile and Jax pulls his wallet out.

"No stripper," Clint grunts pointedly at Jax after Matt pockets the cash.

"Oh, c'mon! Then what the hell are we going to do?"

"Drink and shoot guns on Clint's property," Eric says, climbing the ladder he just hoisted up.

"Can I come?" Matt asks and my chest tightens, knowing he wants to hang out with me and my brothers.

"Sure, as long as your mom's okay with it. Make sure she knows about shooting guns and tell her your grandpa will probably be there, too."

"I'll go ask now." He dashes off looking a lot happier than he did earlier.

"I like that kid," Eric says as he takes a strand of lights from Jax.

"He's perked up," Clint notes.

I slowly come down the ladder. "His dad told him I was leaving, and that the kids were moving in with him. I think he's confused."

"I saw the video Burns took," Eric says, stapling in the lights. "Have you told Amber about it?"

"Not yet, but I will."

"What video?" Jax asks.

"Burns got Henry on video being an idiot," Eric reveals.

"What is up with him and the photo frenzy?" Clint asks, going to Eric's ladder to hold it steady.

"He's becoming nostalgic in his old age." Jax shrugs. "But I might hide his Polaroid before the bachelor party."

"Good plan."

"Luke!" Matt cries excitedly and runs up to me. "Mom said I can go as long as there aren't any strippers."

"Awesome!" I hold out my fist and he pounds it.

"Fork over the cash, buddy, you narc'd on me." Jax holds out his hand.

"Didn't." Matt shakes his head with a smug grin. "I told her there won't be any girls allowed."

"Same thing."

"Is not."

"I'm with the kid." Eric chuckles.

"Me, too." I smile.

"Don't give in," Clint grunts to Matt.

"You all are jackwagons," Jax grumbles.

# 16

## - Amber -

No more night shifts. No more coming home when the kids are waking up. No more trying to sleep during the day and no more night shift bonus pay, but I'm not too worried about that. Thanks to Luke, my expenses haven't been too taxing on my bank account. Hopefully, Sarah will get to the bottom of the insurance claim being rejected and then I can breathe a little easier.

For the first in a long time, I'm excited about how my life is starting to unfold. I'll be on the same sleep schedule as the kids, I have Luke to warm my bed, and Sarah seems to think the custody case will be dropped. Maybe luck is on my side. It's about time because I'm tired of getting knocked down. I just want some peace.

Smiling, I tiptoe into my room, wanting nothing more than to crawl into bed and curl up next to Luke. Only there is one tiny problem with that. Emily is sleeping horizontally in my bed with her legs draped over Luke's stomach.

Quietly, I puff air through my lips and tiptoe past the bed and into the walk-in closet. Luke's work boots and clothes are now hanging on what use to be the empty half of the closet. A few boxes are tucked in the corner and various hats line the top shelf.

I should probably be concerned with Luke moving his stuff into what was just my room— especially without asking me, the cocky bastard. But strangely, I'm not bothered by it. After the weekend we had together, all my doubts have started to become distant memories.

Tugging off my shoes and scrubs, trying to be quiet, two warm hands wrap around my bare waist and my thoughts turn into pure unadulterated desire.

"Mornin'," Luke whispers, nuzzling my ear. "How was your last night shift?"

"Busy." I sigh, leaning back into his chest. "It's always busy this time a year. People are always cooking their Thanksgiving meal in some crazy way that leads to accidents or they're brawling over some popular Christmas toy."

"Hmm."

"You need to stop," I whisper when Luke starts to kiss down my neck to my shoulder, even though I don't want him to.

"Why?" he murmurs, his hand sliding up to cup my breast and my nipples pebble against the fabric of my bra. I wish I had taken it off before he came in.

"We've got a sleeping child a few feet away."

"Right," Luke says, kissing my temple before he pulls away. There's a soft click from the closet door shutting before he's back. "Can you be quiet?"

"I can be quiet."

Luke's hand slips beneath the lace of my panties, my own joining him as my other hand wraps around the nape of his neck.

"Shit, that's hot," Luke whispers, his breath warm against my skin.

His fingers and mine make their way to the apex of my legs. I can feel myself tremble in anticipation before they glide through my folds. "You're soaked," he murmurs as I gasp from the pure pleasure our fingers entice.

Luke releases my breast and wraps his hand around my lower jaw, angling my head so he can claim my mouth and my moan as it claws from my throat.

Following Luke's fingers deeper into my soaked folds, he pushes one finger then two inside. My core pulsates and tingles with every thrust. Luke is hard, his dick is pressing into my bottom in rhythm with our fingers. I can feel the building orgasm tighten around our fingers much quicker than I'd like. Luke feeling it too finds my clit with his thumb and presses down while my fingers slip free and I brace myself.

I'm wound tight and ready to snap as the pressure pools in my core. Luke's fingers swirl inside me, then push deeper as his thumb continues to press down on my clit. I fuck his hand harder before I jerk with the intensity of the orgasm and clamp tight around his fingers in exhausted bliss.

Tremors shot through my body and my legs almost give out when Luke's strong arms wrap around my waist and holds me tight against his chest.

"I love the little noises you make," Luke whispers, his erection hard against my ass. He continues to kiss me, moving down my neck. I let him hold me captive until my strength returns.

I turn in Luke's arms with a sedated smile on my face. "Thank you."

"My pleasure."

"Your turn." I move to push his pants down, but he stops me.

"As much as I want that, I need to get the kids up and get them to school," Luke says taking my hands and bringing them to his lips. "Besides, I wanted to make this about you."

"I should get them up." I sag in his arms, exhaustion wanting to pull me under.

"Let me do it, you need your rest." Luke kisses my cheek then pulls a shirt from his shelf and pulls it over my head.

"Thank you, Luke." I sigh, pushing my arms through the shirt sleeves. "I could use a few hours of sleep. Are you heading to the shop after you drop the kids off?"

"Yeah, but I'll come back here around lunchtime. We have some . . . things to discuss."

"Uh-oh." I step back and search his face. "That doesn't sound good."

"Go sleep, we'll talk at lunch."

"Luke . . .."

"Go." He kisses me, then opens the closet door and pushes me out.

*****

"Is that bacon I smell? I'm starving," I say as I come around the corner into the kitchen and make an abrupt stop. "Eric."

"Afternoon," Eric says over his shoulder, standing over the stove. It's uncanny how similar all the Colson brothers are—monstrously tall with sleek black hair and blue eyes. All similar, yet also different. Luke has a charming smile, Clint's just plain scary, Eric is always serious, and Jax . . . well, Jax just looks wild.

Seeing Eric and his serious glance makes him hard to read. I never know how to act around him.

"I forgot you were here." Maybe small talk will get him to warm up and maybe even crack a smile. "What are you making?"

"BLTs," he grunts before turning the burner off. "I'll be heading out later this afternoon."

"Oh, okay." I plop my head in my hand and watch him scoop out the bacon and place it over a paper towel-covered plate.

"Luke is on his way."

"Okay."

An awkward silence fills the kitchen and I struggle with something to say, but Eric beats me to it. "Coffee?"

"Yes, please." I smile at him, but he just nods and pulls a mug from the cabinet and walks to the coffee maker.

"So . . .."

"I've . . .."

"You go." I laugh, embarrassed and I know it sounds strained.

"Creamer?"

"Yes, please." I suck in a breath before blowing it past my lips. "So, you were saying?"

"Can I crash here for Clint and Dawn's wedding?" Eric asks, pouring a little too much creamer in my coffee then walking it to me.

"Of course, you don't need to ask." I take the coffee and blow on it before taking a sip. "Thank you."

"Would it be too much trouble if I brought my dog Molly?" Eric stares down at me and I get the feeling he talks to everyone as if he's interrogating them.

"Oh um . . . well, I don't mind but you should probably run that by Luke."

"I did, he said it was your call." Eric nods, then pulls a tomato and a head of lettuce from the fridge. "I've been on the road a lot lately, and I don't want to keep asking my guys back home to watch her."

"Your guys?"

"The guys working for me."

"Right." I flash a small smile and again, we are surrounded by awkward silence. "So, tell me about Molly."

"She's a German Shepherd." Eric pulls his phone from his pocket and taps in his code, scrolling through what I think are pictures of her but when he slides it over, it's a video of Luke . . . and Henry? "Luke asked me to show this to you if he didn't get here before you woke up."

"What is this?" I ask and hit play to watch Henry pull some kind of bizarre macho man act on Luke. Did he seriously threaten Luke? "When did this happen?"

"Sunday when he dropped the kids off," Eric says, slicing the tomato as if nothing was wrong.

"And I'm just now finding out?" I put the phone down and slide it back to Eric. "Why didn't he tell me?"

Luckily, I don't have to wait long for the answer. Luke walks through the back door into the kitchen.

"Why didn't you tell me about this?" I get off the stool and point to Eric's phone.

"Good, you've seen it. Sit down, I need to tell you more."

"There's more?" Luke stands in front of me, his hands wrap around my hips, and he pulls me in for a kiss I meant to dodge.

"Henry told the kids they were going to be living with him."

"He did what?" I rip from Luke's hold, glaring up at him. "When?"

"I don't know. Matt told me yesterday."

"Why didn't you tell me this yesterday?" I start to pace the kitchen. "That mother trucker!"

"I was going to tell you, but you were asleep, then everyone was over yesterday. I sent it to Sarah, and she said it could wait until today after you had some rest."

"You should have told me, Luke!"

"I was doing what I thought was best. Sarah asked me to have you call her at noon."

"She's on the phone," Eric interrupts, waving his phone at us.

"Hey guys," Sarah says over the speaker. "Amber, be calm. I told Luke to wait so you could be rested. Give the poor guy a break."

"Whatever." I roll my eyes but don't stop my pacing.

"I reviewed the video, and we can use it against Henry in court. I also sent Henry's lawyer an email letting him know we have evidence of Henry making a threat toward you, Amber, and reminded him that nothing can be said to the children about the upcoming court hearing."

"I told Matt he should talk to Amber about where he wants to live. Will that hurt Amber's case?" *Wait a minute . . . Matt spoke to Luke?*

"You handled it perfectly, Luke. Just tell them that nothing is final, but their voice does matter."

"I can't believe that crud muffin," I mutter, biting my thumbnail.

"It gets worse," Sarah says, and I stop my pacing to stare at the phone. "I spoke with my friend Carl in Wichita who knows insurance law. He spoke with your insurance claim adjuster and learned that Henry had called him. Henry suggested you and Dad were possibly trying to commit fraud."

"What?" I screech at the same time Luke swears under his breath.

"Carl is investigating, but he thinks that he can get your claim overturned. I don't want you to worry about it for now. What I need from you is to help me understand what Henry's up to."

"I have no idea what he's up to. This whole situation is so insane to me," I say feeling helpless.

"I'll do some digging. If Henry's acting out of character, maybe his digital footprint will tell us what's going on," Eric speaks up.

"What do you mean by digital footprint?" Luke asks, the seriousness in his expression a mirror to Eric's.

"I'll look into his financial history, call logs, travel trends, social media presence . . .. It might help paint a picture of what's going on in his life and may give us a clue as to why he's out to ruin Amber."

I look at him confused. "Ruin?"

"He's trying to take your kids from you, he's melding in your fire insurance claim, and now he's threatening to make things more difficult for you if Luke doesn't step out of the picture. Are you seeing a pattern?" Eric asks and for the first time, he doesn't sound so serious but sympathetic.

"Yeah, I guess . . . but why would he try to ruin me? What does he have to gain? It doesn't make any sense."

"I'm with Amber. It doesn't make any sense," Sarah says.

"Maybe he wants to see you suffer," Luke says quietly. "He's jealous."

"Jealousy makes people do stupid shit," Eric agrees.

"He isn't jealous. This all started before you and I were even talking." I put my hands on my hips and let my head fall back, looking up at the ceiling. None of this makes sense.

"Guys, I need to meet with another client in a few minutes. Eric, dig into Henry; we can look over what you find when I'm back in town for the wedding. Amber, Luke, don't do anything that will raise suspicion. Just continue doing what you're doing. We'll get to the bottom of this," Sarah orders, and I nod as if she can see me. "I'll see you guys in two weeks. Bye."

"Bye," I whisper, but she already hung up.

Lady Luck has finally shown her cruel smile at me. All I get is a taste of happiness.

# 17

# - Luke -

"Thanks for lunch," I say to Eric as he gathers his stuff.

"Yeah, no problem," Eric says, then nods toward Amber, who's been silent since the call with Sarah. "I'll dig into Henry. You take care of your girl."

"Yeah, thanks, see you in two weeks." I clamp a hand on his shoulder and pull him in for a hug.

"See you, Amber," Eric calls out over my shoulder.

"Bye, Eric." She waves with a small smile.

I watch Eric walk to his car and load up before I close the door and turn to face Amber. She's still picking at her food.

"You need to eat," I say, coming over to her.

"I'm not hungry." She sighs, getting up from the stool and taking her plate to the sink.

Moving to stand behind her, I wrap my arms around her waist and kiss her neck. When she sags back into my chest, a little bit of the tension in my shoulders relaxes. "I'm sorry I waited so long to tell you what happened."

"It's okay. I know why you did it." She puts her hands over my arms. "But in the future, can you clue me in sooner?"

"Yes." I kiss her neck again.

"I don't know how to sit here and just wait to figure out what Henry's up to," she admits and stares out the window over the sink, looking at nothing in particular.

"Don't try to handle this on your own, Amber. Talking to Henry isn't going to give you the answers you are looking for. You need to let Sarah and Eric do their job."

"I know, but I don't like being . . . useless." She turns in my arms and looks up at me, her emerald eyes full of frustration.

"I know what it's like to have someone come out of nowhere and try to ruin your life. I wouldn't wish it on anyone, especially you, but at least you have a lot of people to help you get through it."

"If I can't confront Henry, then what can I do, just sit around and mope?"

"We have a lot to do on the house . . . flooring to pick out for the bathrooms. Dawn's wedding is in two weeks, so you have a ton of things that will be keeping you busy. Focus on them, and me, and we'll figure this out."

"You're right, I have a lot of things I need to do around here, but at the moment, I can only think of one thing I want to do." Amber fists my shirt and pulls me in for a kiss, and I am more than happy to keep her distracted. I'll burn off all the stress she has if she'll let me.

"How about christening the kitchen?" I guide her around to the island. "Take your pants off."

Amber doesn't protest as she follows my orders while I unbutton my pants and pull them and my boxer briefs down. I gaze down at her perfect body, with her creamy soft skin, so thankful she gave me a second chance. Caressing my fingers down her back before I grab my dick, I stroke myself a couple of times before running it between her folds. She's already soaked, and her juices coat me. I vow to christen every room in this house with her.

I slide in just a little before pulling out, teasing her, and relish the noises she makes. I push in again a little farther and she whimpers. I love that sound and want to hear it again, only Amber has other ideas and pushes back, taking more of me.

I grab her hips and halt her movements for a moment, then thrust hard. She cries out. Such beautiful music to my ears. Cupping one of her breasts under her shirt, I pull down her bra and pinch her nipple. "You feel so fuckin' good," I groan into her ear. She turns her head and smiles at me with lust-filled eyes before rocking back hard. I let her have control, wanting her to feel in control just for a moment during these uncertain times. She maintains a steady rhythm, rocking hard and fast. Her insides clutch tighter and tighter around my dick. My name passes her lips in a breathy moan, and I know she's so close. Moving my hand around her hip to her clit, I circle the bundle of nerves with my fingers.

She rocks harder; I circle faster and flick her nipple knowing all the places she loves me touching. That's when she releases I want it to be explosive. Gripping the island counter tightly, she rocks hard once, twice, and holds, her inside pulsating tight around my dick. She sags, spent by her orgasm, and I take over pounding into her, each thrust taking me closer and closer to release, but I want to hold on just a little longer. I want to savor the feel of her hot and tight around me. A growl deep in my chest climbs its way up my throat. I can't hold back any longer as it erupts, and I come hard.

We stay where we are, not moving, breathing hard, and waiting for our hearts to return to a normal rhythm.

"Keep me busy like that and I'll never stress again," she says, turning her head to look at me. Her emerald eyes are free of stress, and slightly glazed with the last remnants of her orgasm.

"I will gladly take on that task." I kiss her shoulder and pull out of her. She mewls in protest and my dick twitches. "Round two in the shower starts now."

"You don't have to tell me twice."

# Fight Forever

# 18

## - Amber -

Two weeks have gone by, and both Sarah and Eric are expected to arrive tomorrow, hopefully, with some news. So far, they have just reassured me that they are doing everything they can to figure out what Henry is up to, but neither has actually given me any kind of details that would suggest he is up to something.

The waiting is driving me insane and even though Luke has been trying hard to keep me distracted with projects around the house and mind-blowing marathon sex-filled nights, I still can't shake the feeling that the worse has yet to come.

It's taking a toll on me, and people are starting to notice. My new nurse supervisor asked me if I need to take an extra day of vacation to get more adjusted to my new shift just before I clocked out.

"You seem a little more stressed than usual," she casually mentioned, but I could see the worry in her eyes, wondering if she had made the right choice in letting me switch shifts. After reassuring her I was just a little stressed preparing for the wedding this weekend and that I wouldn't let it affect my work, she nodded and told me to have a good weekend.

Collecting my thoughts as I head out to the employee parking lot, I don't even register that someone has been calling my name until Sheriff McKnight taps me on the shoulder.

"Whoa." He steps back when I spin around so fast and let out a little squeak. "You okay?"

"Yeah, sorry, you scared me." I exhale, forcing myself to relax before pasting on a smile. "How can I help you, sheriff?"

"Call me Warren." He smiles as his eyes scan over me. He isn't checking me out but assessing me, reading my body language. I hate that I can so easily be read.

"How can I help you, Warren?"

"Are you sure you're okay?" he asks, eyeing me more suspiciously, hooking his thumbs in his belt loop.

"I've got a lot on my plate right now," I confess, hoping he doesn't try to pry further. I'm not even sure how I would begin to tell him what is really going on in my life, and whether I *should* tell him.

"Can I walk you to your car?" He gestures toward the exit leading to the employee parking lot.

"Oh, uh . . . sure?"

"I don't bite, Amber." Warren chuckles and signals to follow him.

"I know you don't bite." I roll my eyes and follow him out. "I'm sure you have other things to do than walk me to my car."

"I have ulterior motives." Warren winks over at me. "I wanted to see if your sister was going to be at Clint and Dawn's wedding."

"Sarah? Yeah, she's part of the wedding party," I say, side-eyeing him as we maneuver through the cars.

"So, she's coming into town? Does she plan to stay through Christmas?"

"That's the plan." I stop just before we reach my car. "You like my sister?"

"She's a beautiful woman. What's not to like?" Warren smirks down at me.

"I noticed you were on the wedding guest list. I thought you hated the Colson men."

"I never had any issues with Clint or Luke. Eric and Jax were thorns in my side, but that was a long time ago," he says, rocking back on his heels.

"Glad to know my boyfriend is on your good side." I smile, not really believing his word, and pull my keys out of my purse. "Are you wanting me to *invite* you over when Sarah's in town so you can make a move?"

"I wouldn't object to an invite . . .."

"Eric plans to stay with us. Not sure that will work out well." I laugh out loud and walk around the hood of my car to the driver's side. "What the heck?"

"What's the problem?" Warren asks as he comes around to where I'm standing.

I look at him in disbelief. "I think my tires have been slashed."

"What?" He leans down to inspect the large gash in the tire wall of my driver's side tire.

Straightening, he looks around, then bends to look into the car parked next to mine. The windows are tinted, but not so dark that you can't see in, and there appears to be a man sitting in the car. It's running, too. I was so busy talking to Warren that I never even noticed.

Warren walks around it and knocks on the driver's side window. I hesitate for a moment, then come around to see the man sitting behind the wheel. His hair is shaggy and a dirty blonde color that could use a wash. I can't tell his height, but he looks tall since his head is close to hitting the top of his car. Nothing about him is familiar to me, but he glares at me as if he knows me.

"Can I see your license and registration?" Warren asks, stepping in front to block me from the man.

"Why do you need to see it?"

"Why don't you step out of the vehicle?" Warren opens the man's door, but he doesn't let it fully open before tugging on it hard and slamming it shut.

"I wasn't doing anything but sitting here. I don't have to give you shit," he spits out, the sound of his car door locks engaging.

Warren steps back when the man starts to roll his window up and says something into the radio on his shoulder. The man pulls out from the parking spot and when his license plate is visible, Warren reads it into his radio.

"What just happened?" I ask Warren when he finishes talking to whoever is on the other end of his radio.

"Nothing you need to worry about. Let's get your tire changed and I'll follow you home."

"Thanks, Warren, but I can call Luke or my dad to help me. I wouldn't want to waste any more of your time," I say staring at the tire that I know how to change but really don't want to.

"Nonsense. I'll change your tire and maybe you can help me make a good impression on your sister," Warren says as he rolls up his shirt sleeves. "Can you pop your trunk?"

"Two things wrong with that." I chuckle, hitting the trunk button on my key fob. "First, Eric has made his claim on her, and I need to play nice with Eric."

"And the second reason?" Warren smiles big at me, pushing the trunk lid up and lifting the carpet covering my spare tire.

"Second, she lives on the East Coast. Why would you want to start a long-distance relationship with someone who lives so far away, and I think who may be still hung up on Eric?"

"Do you really believe Sarah is still hung up over Eric?" he asks, pulling the jack and spare out of the trunk as if it weighs nothing.

"Those two have history, you know that."

"I do, but that doesn't mean they have a future." He kneels by the slashed tire.

I kneel next to him. "You are putting me in a very precarious position."

"Nah, I'm just stacking the deck." He winks and gets to work on changing my tire.

\*\*\*\*\*

"Amber, finally! What took you so long?" Sarah greets me as I come through the back door. The excited smile on her face puts me on high alert as she leads me through the kitchen toward the living room.

"Sorry I had . . .. Wait, who are you?" I ask the strange Thor-like man dressed in a milkman costume standing by the couch next to an over-eager looking Jax.

"He's Dawn's wedding present," Jax says with a wild smile on his face.

"Wedding present?"

"Oh, dear, don't be daft." Miss Janet sighs as she pours what I suspect is a margarita into a cup and hands it to me.

"Is he—"

"A stripper?" Jax finishes my sentence. "Yes, he is. You're welcome."

"Clint is going to be so pissed." Sarah laughs. "You better hope he doesn't find out, Jax."

"My brother will be thanking me after he's done." Jax thumbs to the stripper, winking over at Dawn, who blushes.

"Your funeral," Dawn murmurs and Jax's smile falters.

"I best be going. You ladies enjoy your evening." Jax back-pedals to the front door.

"Where is Emily and Matt?" I ask my mom, who is pulling several dollar bills from her purse. Where in the world did she get so many dollar bills?

"Luke took Emily to Mrs. Barley's for a tea party, and Matt went with him to Clint's for the bachelor party," my mom says, then grabs her drink and points to Milkman Thor and waves her money. "Dance, hottie, dance."

"Oh, good Lord," I mutter, looking at a wide-eyed Dawn before taking a big gulp from my margarita. If I have to help babysit my mom and Miss Janet, I'm going to need a lot more alcohol.

"Let's get this party started!" Miss Janet waves for us to follow as she sashays to the couch where she places a giant pitcher of margaritas on the coffee table and squeals like a teenage girl trapped in an eighty-year-old body.

"There is still time. We can slip out the back," I whisper.

"No one is going anywhere." Sarah looks between me and Dawn. "This is Dawn's bachelorette party. If she can't drink, she can at least shove a wad of cash down this hunk of a man's banana hammock."

"She's got a point." I shrug at Dawn, who looks mortified.

"I'll look, but no touching." She rolls her eyes, rubbing her small pregnant belly and I can't help but laugh.

"Don't worry, dears. I'll do all the touching for you," Miss Janet hollers from the living room, dancing in her seat and literally drooling.

Music from a speaker Milkman Thor brought clicks on and my mom whistles as we all take seats on the couch.

"Who's ready to party, ladies?" Milkman Thor asks, then tears his clothes off and my mom goes nuts.

I need more to drink.

# 19

## - Luke -

Amber is stunning in her light pink bridesmaid dress. Emily and Sarah are wearing matching dresses, but the dress was made for Amber. Her curves are softened by the floor-length design, but her breasts peek out and I openly check her out with no shame.

Walking down the aisle with her is much different than the last time we were paired together for a wedding. For starters, her smiles are genuine and every time she looks at me with the warmth and happiness she has for her friend

Dawn, my chest tightens. I picture us walking together and her warmth and happiness is for us.

I only have eyes for Amber as my brother and Dawn say their vows. When our eyes met, I swear she reads my mind and her smile spreads farther across her beautiful face, though she tried to hide it. I nearly interrupted the wedding so I could get down on one knee and ask her right then and there, but I'm certain Clint would have murdered me. Amber would help bury my body for ruining Dawn's day, and I would never get my wedding day with her.

Besides, I need to be patient with Amber. Things are good between us, but she needs time to get used to us having a future. Plus, we still need to figure out what Henry is up to. The last thing I want to do is add more stress to her life.

Watching Amber now chatting with her family at the reception, my patience to slip a ring on her finger wavers. At least I have her next to me in our—yes, *our*— bed because I'm not letting it be just her bed or mine. We're together for better or worse, even if she hasn't figured that out yet.

"Who the hell invited that jackass?" Eric hisses when he hears Sarah laugh at something Sheriff McKnight says to her.

"He's not so bad." I shrug. "He helped Dawn and Clint when her ex blew into town."

"It's his job to help people, that doesn't make him a damn saint," Eric growls then heads for the bar where Sarah and McKnight are chatting.

"Eric has his hands full with your sister. What is going on between those two?" I ask Amber when I take a seat next to her.

"Warren is staking a claim." Amber giggles, watching as Eric pulls Sarah away from McKnight.

I raise a brow at her. "Warren?"

"He asked me to call him Warren." Amber shrugs as Emily climbs off her lap and into mine.

"Are you going to dance with my mommy?" Emily whispers loud enough for Amber to hear.

"Absolutely, little human." I smile over at Amber.

"Not until this mommy gets some champagne." Amber winks, then stands and heads over to the bar.

"Hey, Matt, looking good in that suit," Clint says, holding his fist out.

"Thanks," Matt mumbles then fist bumps Clint. Matt is really breaking out of his shell. He was fun at the bachelor party, even without having anyone his age to hang out with. We have really started to bond.

Despite the looming custody hearing and Henry's recent threats, everything is falling into place. Amber isn't resisting me, the kids like me, and the house is nearly complete.

"You look handsome," Dawn says. She places her hands around his face and kisses his forehead. A deep blush colors Matt's face, and I bite back a chuckle.

"This place looks great," I tell the happy couple when they sit with us. *Benny's Bar* was transformed into a reception once again, but there are fewer tables and a smaller buffet, making the space feel more intimate and less crowded— exactly the way Clint and Dawn wanted it.

"Thanks, brother," Clint grunts, wrapping an arm around Dawn, who hasn't stopped smiling since she walked down the aisle.

Jax falls into the chair next to Dawn. "Whose idea was it to invite McKnight?"

"Mine." Dawn looks over at my little brother.

"You're brilliant." Jax smiles and leans over to kiss her cheek. "Personally, I can't stand the guy, but I love watching Eric lose his shit."

"Keep your paws off my wife," Clint growls, pulling Dawn closer to his side.

Dawn looks around confused. "Why's he going to lose it?"

"McKnight and Eric have been bitter enemies since high school, and it all started over a girl." Jax smirks over his glass of whiskey. "That girl being Sarah."

"Oh no . . .." Dawn looks worried and glances at Clint.

"Shut it, Jax," Clint grunts and shoves Jax.

"Speaking of Eric, where did he and Sarah run off to?" I ask, glancing around for the couple.

"If he's lucky, making up for lost time." Jax snickers.

"Children," Amber says and smacks the back of Jax's head as she comes around the table to take a seat.

"Sorry, pipsqueak," Jax says, raising his glass to Emily then Matt.

"I'm not a pipsqueak, I'm a little human," Emily says and lays her head on my shoulder.

"Sorry, little human." Jax nods, smiling at my girl.

"Are you getting tired?" Amber asks as she runs a hand over Emily's head.

"No," she says around a yawn.

"I'm going to see if Linda needs any help packing up the food," Dawn says to Clint, who tugs her back toward him and kisses her so passionately, it even makes me blush.

"I'll help." Amber chuckles and stands, finishing her champagne and places the glass down.

"Where's my kiss?" I snag her wrist. Amber's smile is radiant, taking my breath away. Leaning forward, she kisses the corner of my mouth.

I notice McKnight look around before he heads over to our table. "Has anyone seen Sarah?"

"She's over there," Matt says, nodding toward Benny's office.

"Thanks," McKnight says and pats Matt's shoulder before extending his hand out to Clint. "Best wishes."

Clint stands and shakes his hand. "Thanks for coming."

Nodding at us, he turns and heads toward Sarah, who looks a little disheveled in her wrinkled bridesmaid dress. Her hair has fallen out of its updo and a flush brightens her cheeks.

While Sarah is talking to McKnight, Eric emerges from Benny's office, tucking his shirt into his pants before running his hands through his hair.

Eric narrows his eyes, looking pissed when he sees Sarah hug McKnight, but he walks past them and steals the whiskey out of Jax's hand and gulps it down.

"You're looking . . . relaxed," Clint says, and we all bust up laughing.

"You all are a bunch of assholes," Eric grumbles, looking into the empty whiskey glass.

"Children," Jax reprimands and smacks the back of Eric's head.

Matt chuckles then yawns. I need to get these kids home soon.

"Where are Amber and Dawn?" Sarah asks, coming over to the table and taking a seat as far away from Eric as possible.

"Helping Linda pack up," Clint answers and stands from the table. "Thanks for coming everyone, but I have somewhere to be."

"I'm going to go find Burns and Janet and get those crazy kids home before they find an empty office and do something naughty." Jax stands and buttons his jacket.

"Shut it, Jax," Eric says, punching Jax in the gut.

"Asshole," Jax wheezes and walks away, winking at Sarah, who rolls her eyes.

"Matt, do you mind checking to see if your mom is ready to go?" Sarah asks Matt, who yawns again but nods, then slowly gets up and walks off.

"Eric, were you able to find anything out about Henry?" Sarah asks after Matt is out of earshot.

"His new wife filed for divorce a few weeks ago. But other than that, he's clean." Eric rubs his chin looking pissed.

"We should talk about this with Amber." I glance over at the kitchen where Amber is saying goodbye to her parents.

"I'll be over tomorrow, and we can talk more." Sarah nods, then gets up and glances quickly at Eric.

Eric stares at Sarah intently. "How are you getting home?"

"I'm . . ." Sarah clears her throat then points over her back, "getting a ride with my parents."

"Good." Eric nods, stands, and then stalks away, rubbing the back of his neck.

"I'm such an idiot," Sarah groans as she watches Eric walk out the door.

"Nah." I chuckle, standing up and shifting a sleeping Emily in my arms. "But be careful with him. He's tender-hearted under that thick skin of his."

"I know." She sighs with a sympathetic smile. "Get your family home, we'll talk tomorrow."

Yes, I'll take my family home. Happily.

*****

"How's my pretty girl?" Eric coos when his German Shepperd Molly greets us as we walk into the house.

"Ah, you're such a good doggie daddy," Amber coos at Eric with a laugh.

"Can Molly sleep with me?" Matt asks, getting down on his knees to scratch Molly's ears.

"Sure, if you're mom's okay with it," Eric says, patting Matt's head.

Amber shrugs, kissing the top of Matt's head. "I'm okay with it."

"I must warn you, Molly is a bed hog," Eric says, taking his suit jacket off and throwing it over his shoulder. "And she snores."

"Awesome." Matt smiles at Eric then pats his leg. "C'mon, Molly, time for bed."

"I'll put Emily to bed," Amber offers, holding her arms out take Emily.

"I'll carry her up." I shake my head, then look over at Eric. "Can you lock up?"

"Sure." Eric walks to the door and throws the latch as Amber follows me up the stairs.

We quickly work together to get Emily out of her flower girl dress and into her pajamas, tucking her in without her waking, and silently leave her bedroom.

"I've been waiting all night to get this dress off you," I whisper to Amber outside Emily's bedroom.

"Then you better hurry and get me downstairs," she whispers back before casually walking down the stairs.

"Not fast enough." I rush down the stairs and grab her around the waist. We make a quiet, yet mad dash down the stairs, through the hallway, and into our bedroom before clicking the door shut.

"Clothes off, now," I growl, pulling off my jacket and kicking off my shoes.

Amber slowly turns around and pulls her hair to the side. "Unzip me." I would love to pull her zipper down with my teeth, but I want her naked more.

The zipper takes no time to unzip, but I take my time running my hands up her back, watching her shiver as they make their way to her dress straps. Sliding one, then the other off her shoulders until it falls to the floor, she stands in nothing but a lace thong.

I have seen Amber, all of her, up-close and personal many times, and every time it takes my breath away. Every. Fucking. Time.

"Are you going to just stare at me?" Amber looks at me over her shoulder with a flirty grin.

"Yes." I nod, then rip the rest of my clothes off. They could be tattered remains for all I care.

I grab her hips and pull her back into my chest. I slowly pull down her thong, kissing a trail down her back, and smile when I feel her tremble. When she steps out of them, she turns and I kiss my way up her stomach until I reach those delicious tits she had peeking out at me all night. I grab her ass and lift her up, and her legs wrap around my waist. Walking us to the bed, I don't lay her down; instead, I sit exploring her soft skin, memorizing every inch, every little freckle.

My mouth hovers over one of her hard nipples before I kiss it once, then move to the other and kiss it too. Her hands comb through my hair as her head falls back for better access.

"So beautiful," I whisper against her skin then look up at her. She's peering down at me with eyes so black with lust. "And all *mine*."

I don't give her time to protest. I suck in one of her nipples and lick around it, wanting to suck every ounce of pleasure from her.

Amber grinds against my dick that throbs with need to be inside her.

"I need you inside me now," she pants. I don't want this to be fast; I want to make love to her. I want her to feel my love, accept it, and trust it.

"No," I say, releasing her breast and attacking the other, biting softly. She lets out a moan and decides to take matters into her own hands. Grabbing my dick, I almost blow in her hand before she presses it against her entrance and comes done hard.

"*Fuck!*" I hiss, grabbing her hips and stopping her movements. "I need a moment."

"Can't stop . . .." She tries to move but I flip her onto her back.

"So bossy." I smile down at her.

"Luke, I swear if you don't move *now*, I'm going to—"

"What?" I chuckle, pulling out of her and she whimpers.

"*Please*," she whines, lifting her hips and her arms grab my biceps. I want to plow into her, but not yet.

"I want to make love to you," I tell her, and she jerks her head up, her lust-filled eyes searching mine.

"Let me make love to you," I whisper across her lips and slowly ease inside her. She accepts all of me with a sigh that is music to my ears.

My movements are slow at first until she rocks her hips along with me, and the way her eyes stare back at me so intently, I know she's making love to me, too.

*I love you.*

It's at the tip of my tongue. I want to say it but instead, I kiss her passionately until our movements speed up and her insides tighten around me. She holds me tighter; her thighs pull me deeper until she breaks our kiss and her orgasm rips through her. She moans my name and I lose it, pumping hard until I release inside her, biting back the words I so badly want to say.

*I love you.*

I think I can see the words in her eyes. I felt it when she made love to me and moaned my name but saying them now would only freak her out, and I can't take us two steps back when I finally got us one step closer to forever.

# 20

# - Amber -

"Henry's getting a divorce," I repeat what Eric just shared with us moments ago. "Was he sleeping with a younger, richer woman?"

"Not that I can tell, but he is shifting money around. Probably trying to hold onto whatever he can of DeeDee's fortune," Eric says over his coffee cup.

"What does that have to do with me?" I ask, glancing out the back door to make sure the kids are still playing outside with Molly.

"It may be why he's trying to get the kids; why he's trying to ruin you." Eric shrugs.

"It doesn't seem likely," Sarah says, looking as frustrated as I am. Sarah and Eric have both been hard at work trying to understand Henry's motives, but so far, nothing adds up.

"So, you don't have anything on Henry? Nothing that points to what he is up to?" Luke directs his question at Eric, who glares at his brother. The two have been pestering each other since Eric's arrival. Luke has missed his brothers over the years and having them around more has made him happy. His blue eyes get bright with excitement when they come around. He is always asking them to come over or he goes to do something with them. He's going to miss Eric when he heads back to Texas.

I always thought Eric was a quiet person but around his brothers, he breaks out of his shell a little bit. He may act bulletproof but underneath that armor is a softy. I see his soft side whenever the kids are around, but mostly, I see it when Sarah is around. I don't think he ever stopped loving her. I'm starting to wonder if she ever stopped loving him, either.

"I've only had a few weeks to look into this, but what I have uncovered doesn't point to why he would be seeking out to ruin Amber. It would make more sense if he went after his wife." Eric narrows his eyes at Luke, obviously offended that his brother dared to question his abilities.

"What about his involvement with the fire claim?" Luke presses on.

"As far as I can tell, he only reached out the one time and hasn't made contact since."

"This is so frustrating." I cover my face with my hands. "So, we are back to square one."

"I know, I'm sorry." Sarah rubs a hand up and down my back. I'm so thankful she is here right now. Even though she makes a point to visit often, I miss her like crazy and I don't know how I would be able to get through all this drama if she wasn't leading the charge. "But don't worry, he isn't going to get custody of the kids, and Carl thinks he has enough evidence to get the insurance denial overturned."

"I just want this over with," I say, looking up at her.

"I've brought donuts," Jax says, walking through the front door, completely unaware of the heavy conversation we're are having, "and company."

"Morning," Warren greets from behind Jax, wearing his sheriff's uniform and a smile aimed only at Sarah.

*Well this just got interesting.*

"What are you doing here?" Eric asks through clenched teeth and if I wasn't so annoyed over the whole Henry mess, I might've enjoyed the territory spats those two get into whenever my sister is around.

"I came to check on Amber." Warren nods toward me then smiles at Sarah. "And see Sarah."

"Check on Amber?" Luke glances between me and Warren.

"She had a flat the other day, and the man parked next to her car was spotted half a block from your house recently. The officer who reported it was on duty when I called the plates in," Warren tells us, then points to the coffee pot. "Do you mind?"

"Yes, let me get you a mug," I say, getting up and walking around the island. I completely forgot about the flat tire. Things got a bit spicy when I got home that night, and I completely forgot about it.

"What flat tire?" Luke asks as he stands and follows me to the cabinet, reaching over my head to pull down a mug.

"Umm, I forgot to tell you . . . but it's no big deal. I'll handle it later," I try to sound casual. "My tire may have been slashed on Friday."

"May have been?" Luke glares down at me.

"Well, we don't know for sure, right?" I glance at McKnight for assistance, but he only shrugs.

"How do you forget a tire being *maybe* slashed?" Luke demands, not trying to hide the anger in his tone.

"I . . . I got distracted when I got home," I hesitate to answer before glancing over at Sarah then Jax, who wiggles his eyebrows at me. Of course, Jax isn't going to come to my rescue, he loves to see people squirm.

"With what? And why didn't you call me to come help you with it?" Luke's nostrils flare.

"Warren helped me change it."

"You still should have called me."

"I got home late, and you already left for Clint's bachelor party," I try to explain but hear Luke swear under his breath. "I didn't want to bother you since Warren was there to help."

"You should have called," Luke says, pressing his lips together. "What was so distracting?"

"Yeah, Jax, what was so distracting?" Sarah cuts in, smiling like the cat who ate the canary at Jax.

"From what I heard, you ladies were happy with my *distraction*." Jax smirks back, a half-eaten donut in his hand.

"I hate to interrupt—"

"Shut it, McKnight," Eric snarls, then looks at Jax. "What the hell did you do?"

"Relax. I just got Dawn an early wedding present is all." He takes another bite, nearly stuffing the rest of the donut into his mouth.

"What kind of present?" Luke demands, putting a hand on my waist so I can't go anywhere. Yep, he's going to be even more mad in a minute.

"A stripper?" I wince when it sounds more like a question.

"Fucking hell," Eric swears then glares at Sarah.

"What? I didn't do anything." Sarah looks away from Eric then looks at Warren. "I think we need to get back on topic here, right, Warren?"

"I don't know . . .. I kind of want to hear more about the stripper. Was it a cop or a package delivery man?" Warren winks at Sarah, earning him a scathing glare from Eric.

"It was a milkman," Jax answers.

"Not helping," I mutter at him.

Eric swears under his breath and takes a step closer to Sarah, which only makes Warren chuckle before shifting his eyes to Luke.

"Amber's tire appeared to be slashed, and the man parked next to her claimed he didn't see anything, but he wasn't exactly cooperative," Warren explains, then pulls his notepad out and glances at his notes. "He was spotted parked just half a block from your house, but when officers tried to approach him, he took off. The plates to the car are registered to Arnold Toppler. Would you happen to know this man?"

"Arnold Toppler?" I repeat, glancing at Luke then Sarah. "I've never heard of him before."

"Can you give me the license plate number?" Eric asks Warren, who swivels his eyes to Eric only for a moment before turning his attention back to me.

"Could he have been a patient of yours?" Warren asks, ignoring Eric's request.

"I'd have to look, but he doesn't sound familiar and I didn't recognize him when I first saw him." I shake my head, wracking my brain for some sort of clue who the man is. "You think he may have slashed my tire?"

"I can't say for sure, but I don't like coincidences," Warren replies, snapping his notebook shut and tucking it into his shirt pocket. "We'll see if the hospital has anything on their security cameras, and I'll get back in touch if I find anything out."

I nod. "Thank you, Warren."

"Just doing my job. If you need to get a hold of me, here's my card," Warren says, taking a card and handing it to me. Before I can grab it, Eric snatches it from Warren and pockets it.

"I'll be in touch, McKnight. I want that license plate number," Eric sneers at the man but Warren doesn't flinch. He just nods at me, then turns to Sarah.

"Mind walking me out?" he says to her and she nods, standing from her stool and follows Warren to the door.

"Am I missing something here?" Jax asks, pointing around at us all.

"We think Amber's ex is trying to ruin her and take the kids," Luke shares with Jax, who straightens, losing his wild and carefree expression. Jax may come across as a fun-loving guy without a care in the world, but he cares deeply and most don't see that side of him. I think he's too scared to let anyone get close. At such a young age he watched the most important people in his life die, fade, and leave.

"No shit," he mutters, then looks at Eric. "You're looking into this?"

"Yeah," Eric grumbles, watching the front door where Sarah and Warren are having a quiet conversation. "We didn't have much until McKnight dropped a lead."

"Let me know if you need my help with anything."

"Are you planning to stick around?" Luke asks, reaching around me for a donut.

"Yeah, I think I'll stick around. I spoke with Benny some more last night, and he's serious about selling the bar."

"The fire put a strain on my parents' retirement. They aren't hurting, but they don't want their money tied up in their business in case anything happens to them. They want to put away a nest egg that can't be easily lost," I say feeling shitty. Even though the fire wasn't my fault, Henry's interference is.

"Stop blaming yourself," Luke whispers into my ear, reading my mind and pulling my back against his chest.

"Here," Sarah says, handing Eric a piece of paper. "It's the license plate number you asked for. You're welcome."

Taking the paper, Eric grumbles, "Thank you."

"Can you try to play nice with Warren?" Sarah asks, and I choke on a laugh before covering it with a bite of my donut.

"I will when he stops flirting with you."

"He doesn't flirt with me." Sara shrugs. "We are just friends."

"Mom, I'm hungry," Emily says, coming through the back door.

"Me too," Matt says, letting Molly in before coming through the door.

"Jax brought donuts." I smile at them. "Put your coats up and come help yourself before Jax eats them all."

"Clint and Dawn just pulled in," Matt tells us as he takes off his jacket and heads for the donuts.

"No one tell Clint about the stripper," Jax warns, looking at us all.

"What's a stripper?" Emily asks right as Clint and Dawn walk through the front door. Clint narrows his eyes at us, then looks at Dawn, who tries to smile innocently at her new husband.

"It's a—" Jax starts to whisper to the kids.

"Shut it, Jax!" everyone says at once.

"Little humans, go turn on some cartoons," Luke says in his giant voice that Emily loves as he lifts her so she can reach the donuts.

"We aren't supposed to eat on the furniture, Giant Luke," Emily says when Luke sits her down, then lowers voice. "Unless Mommy isn't here."

"Sit on the floor, little humans," Luke says, losing the giant voice.

"We'll talk about that later," I whisper.

"Sure, after we talk about the stripper."

"You boys are nothing but trouble," Dawn says, coming to the island glowing. I'm so happy for her and Clint. Her life was not easy, and she had to overcome a lot before getting here. I envy the absolute trust she has in Clint and their future together. Luke has made me happier than I have been in a long time, and after last night, I realized I do trust him, but I'm holding myself back from really diving in deep with him. I keep waiting for the other shoe to drop and I'm scared that feeling may never go away.

"And it's your honeymoon. What are you doing here?" Sarah asks as she gives Dawn a hug.

"We thought we would stop by before we head to Kansas City," Clint grunts, reaching over for a donut. Clint was never a man of many words and before Dawn came to Peak Valley, he was reclusive and avoided everyone. The residents of Peak Valley grew scared of him over the years. His sheer size wards people away and no one ever saw his gentleness. Not until Dawn came along. "When are you fools heading out?"

"I'm sticking around for a few weeks," Eric answers, looking at his phone and plugging in the license plate number Sarah had handed him.

"Same," Jax says.

"We should have Christmas dinner together," Dawn suggests, her smile radiant.

"The kids go to Henry's this Friday, and we get them back the day before Christmas Eve," I share, glancing at Sarah. "How long will you be in town?"

"I thought I would stay until after Christmas," she says not looking at Eric, who quickly looks up at her. I take it he didn't expect her to be around, but the corners of his mouth tick up just a fraction.

"Great." Luke claps his hands around my shoulder, his excitement vibrating through me.

"How about a Christmas Day breakfast instead of dinner?"

"Are we doing presents?" Jax asks, looking around at his brothers. "If we are, I need ideas . . .. I just got the kids something."

Shocked, I glance at Jax. "You did?"

"Was I not supposed to?"

"No. I mean, that was nice of you." I smile at him thoughtfully before I realize who I'm talking to. "Wait . . . what did you get them?"

"Bikes," he says softly with a big smile on his face, then looks over his shoulder where the kids are watching TV to make sure they didn't hear him. "Why? What did you think I got them?"

"I don't know . . . something explosive, dangerous, possibly deadly." I shrug then smile at him.

"Matt's bike has a motor," Jax says nonchalantly.

"You got him a motorcycle?" I nearly screech, then look over at the kids, who are eyeing me as if I'm a weirdo.

"Seriously, Jax, a motorcycle?" I ask again, much more quietly.

"Relax. It's a dirt bike, it doesn't go very fast . . . it's perfectly safe," he murmurs, but it does nothing to reassure me. A dirt bike. What was he thinking? Matt could hurt himself. He's far too young for a motorized vehicle.

"I got Matt a helmet to go with the dirt bike," Clint says, clearly not seeing the dangers the Colson men are trying to put my son in.

"I got him some riding gear," Eric chimes in.

"I'm sorry." Dawn frowns at me. "I thought you knew. Luke said it was fine."

I turn to glare at him. "You did *what?*"

His eyes widen and he takes a step back. "He told me he wanted one." Luke puts his hands on my hips. "When the guys asked what to get the kids, I thought bikes would be a great idea since they lost theirs in the fire. Jax found a good deal on a used dirt bike. Clint is going to help get it up and running, and I know Matt has been wanting one. He told us at the bachelor party. A couple of his friends have them, and he told me how he was saving his money for one."

"He is?"

"I will teach him how to ride it and make sure he wears his gear," Luke reassures, pulling me into his chest and kissing my forehead.

"Okay." I nod, though not fully committed to the idea. Luke taking an interest in what Matt wants and making sure he's safe comforts me. I've come to trust him when it comes to Emily and Matt. He is devoted to them like he was devoted to taking care of his brothers, but a mother will always worry.

"Okay?" Luke raises a skeptical brow.

"I trust you, and your brothers . . .. Well, Jax is questionable, but I know you all won't let anything happen to Matt," I say and Luke's eyes spark with emotion—the same emotion I saw spark last night when he insisted we make love. I'm not sure I'm ready to admit what it means, but it still causes my heart to skip a beat and fill me with hope.

"We're going to head out," Clint says, and Luke looks away. "We'll be back for Christmas breakfast."

"Yes, Christmas breakfast." I nod and step away from Luke to hug Dawn.

"Funny, isn't it?" she whispers in my ear.

"What is?"

"Realizing you can have a happy ending."

I squeeze her again, wishing her words were true, while that nagging pit in my stomach twists with unease.

# Fight Forever

# 21

## - Luke -

The first time seeing Emily and Matt leave with Henry was annoying. The second time was upsetting. This time it feels like a piece of my heart is being taken away.

I know *he* is their father, and on some level, I know he won't hurt them directly, but in my gut, I know he plans to hurt their mom and that will hurt them.

Since learning about Arnold Toppler and Henry's pending divorce, keeping the kids and

Amber close has been my sole focus, and to my surprise, Amber hasn't objected.

I expected her to throw a fit when I insisted on taking the kids to school and her to work, but she agreed. She's letting me be more involved and be part of her and the kids' lives, instead of someone on the outside looking in. I'm soaking it up, loving every minute of it, which makes it hard not to tell her I love her, especially at night when she gives me more of herself.

"What are you thinking so hard about?" Amber asks as she snuggles into my side while we watch some medical drama she wanted to watch.

"The kids," I murmur into her hair softly, still debating whether she's ready to hear what she already knows—that she means something to me.

"Are you worried about them being with Henry?" She shifts at my side and looks up at me. Those emerald eyes will be my undoing. I'm not sure I can bite the words back much longer.

"Yeah," I say, brushing a strand of her hair from her temple. I am worried about them. Henry was uncharacteristically happy when he picked the kids up. Not once did he seem hostile or confrontational. "Did he seem . . . weird to you?"

"He seemed happy for a man about to get divorced, but he was happy during our divorce, so maybe he is seeing someone else."

"He was happy about the divorce?" I never did get all the details, only that he cheated.

"He had a beautiful rich woman waiting for him. I can't say I was happy going through the divorce, but I was relieved. He didn't fight for custody then and wasn't opposed to me moving back here. He just wanted everything to be finalized as quickly as possible. He let me have whatever I wanted, not that I wanted much, just the kids."

"If he didn't fight you for custody then, why now?" I ask, not really expecting an answer.

"That's the million-dollar question." Amber sighs, then places a hand on my cheek, studying my face.

"Why are you so calm all of a sudden?" I blurt out.

"I wouldn't exactly call myself calm; I still have my freak-out moments. I want all of this to be over with, but I think having Sarah around telling me I have nothing to worry about helps. Plus, you keep me sane."

"I help keep you sane?" I chuckle because not that long ago, I was one more source of stress for her. It says a lot about what we have managed to overcome.

"I know I haven't been the easiest to deal with, but you're growing on me. I like where we are in this relationship." She squeezes my waist then shifts into my side. "You make an excellent distraction."

*Distraction?*

"What do you mean by distraction?" I ask casually, even though the word gives me a bitter taste in my mouth. Amber may have stopped fighting the connection we have, but she's still holding back.

"You've helped keep me distracted from the crap I'm dealing with." Sensing my unease, she sits up and I feel the loss of her warmth.

"I want to be more than a distraction." I shift in my seat and face her so I can read every emotion that crosses it. Amber always was an open book when it came to her emotions. Her transparency is like a breath of fresh air. I never have to question her motives—even when she isn't telling me how she really feels—it's there in the open for me to see. I would have given up on us long ago if I couldn't read her so easily, but in this moment, I wonder if I haven't been reading her as well as I thought.

"I know," she says with a mixture of confusion in her emerald eyes.

"Then what's holding you back?" I don't want to be confrontational with her—she has enough on her plate—but I need to know the answer. I know I'm not chasing after hopeless dreams, but if I want to fix us. I need to know how to repair the damage I had caused, and only she can give me the answer.

"I'm not holding back."

"I know you want to be with me, but you still keep me at arm's length. Do you not trust me?" I rub a hand down my face and stand, not happy she brushed off my question. Maybe I'm being too sensitive; things between us are good but I don't want complacency, I want Amber, unafraid, fully vested, and committed. I can take this relationship slow if that is what she wants, but not if she keeps waiting for it to crash and burn.

"I trust you." She stands, putting a hand on my back and I swirl around, unable to stop the stream of words that come out of my mouth.

"I love you," I growl, then grab her face in my hands tenderly despite the growing tension in my shoulders. "I *love* you."

"I . . . I know," Amber says, her eyes wide with worry.

"But you don't love me?"

"Luke," she hesitates, then lays her hands on my forearms.

"Just tell me what is holding you back." I squeeze my eyes shut and lean my forehead against hers.

"I'm scared," Amber says softly and steps closer into my space. Slowly, her hands wrap around my waist as she lays her head against my chest. All I have ever wanted was for her to embrace me like this, in this home—*our* home— and promise me forever. "I'm scared to death of telling you how I feel. I'm scared once I do, I'll lose you."

"You will never lose me," I reassure, wrapping my arms around her and breathing just a little bit easier. "Why do you think you'll lose me?"

"Relationships haven't worked out for me. Every time they get *good,* something happens. Something I have no control over, and they end, leaving me even more broken. Right now, my life is a mess. Having you here by my side has made it less messy. I'm scared it's going to end, so I've been holding back. Waiting for you to change your mind, or Henry do something that will make you walk away. I know that sounds crazy, but it's the truth."

"I'm not going anywhere. How do I prove that to you?"

"Keep telling me you aren't going anywhere. Keep showing my kids they are important to you. Keep being you."

"I think I can handle that." I smile into her hair, kissing the top of her head. The tension in my shoulders relaxes some, but there is still a weight on them I don't think will go away until I make Amber mine in the 'put a ring on it' kind of way.

Amber tilts her head up and lifts on her toes, kissing my lips tentatively. She's still worried. Worried our relationship will fall apart, worried she will lose the kids. She needs security, and I know in that moment that I can and will give that to her. I'll find a way so she never has to worry about our relationship ever again.

"I love you," I whisper over her lips before I kiss them, tasting the words on her mouth.

"Prove it," she whispers with a smile.

She may have not told me she loves me back, but I will gladly prove my love to her until she's consumed by it.

Fight Forever

# 22

## - Amber -

The beeping sound of a phone pulls me from the most sedated deep sleep I've had in years. I don't want to move, not when I feel Luke's warm body curled around me.

"Who the fuck is calling you?" Luke mumbles in my ear.

"It's your phone," I groan when the phone continues to ring. Isn't voicemail automatically setup now?

"Fuck." He rolls away from me, taking the warmth with him. "Yeah?"

Luke is silent for several seconds before he throws the covers off and climbs out of bed. "You're there now?"

Now fully awake, I sit up and watch Luke hold his phone to his ear with his shoulder while trying to pull on a pair of his boxer briefs.

"Yeah, I'm on my way," he says into the phone, then clicks it off and tosses it onto the bed.

I rub my eyes. "What's going on?"

"That was Sheriff McKnight. He said there was a break-in at my shop." Luke throws on a shirt and pulls his arms through. "I need to get over there."

"Okay." I nod and climb out of bed, looking on the floor where Luke and I left a trail of clothes.

"No, stay here and sleep." Luke comes to where I'm fishing for my panties and guides me back into bed.

"I want to help."

"I want you to stay here," he says, running a hand down his face, something he does when he's worried and right now, he looks conflicted. "I want you to stay here." He leaves the room, heading for the guest room next door where Eric is staying.

I get up and quickly pull on some clothes, straining to hear the muffled conversation he's having with Eric, but he returns before I'm fully dressed.

"I want you to stay here . . . please," Luke says and again leads me to the bed, picking up his shirt from earlier, peeling mine off, and throwing his over my head. "Eric is here, and I'd feel better if you stayed here where I know you're safe."

"But—"

"There isn't anything you can do there. You'd be in the way, and I would worry about you. Please, just stay here."

"Fine." I sigh, knowing he's probably right. I wouldn't be much help to him.

"Sarah's here." I can hear the smile in his voice though it's difficult to see his face in the darkness.

"She is?" I whisper, looking toward the open door that leads out to the hallway—not that I could see into Eric's room.

"Go back to sleep. I'll be home when you wake, and then we can tease them both over breakfast." Luke kisses my forehead and disappears into the closet, walking out seconds later with a sweatshirt and his work boots.

"Be safe," I say as he's about to leave, but he stops putting on his boots and sweatshirt and stalks back to me.

"I'll be safe," he says, pushing me to lay down then hovers above me. "I've got the woman I love waiting here for me." His mouth slams into mine, kissing away my worry and making my heart skip.

I'm not ready for his mouth to leave mine but I know he is needed elsewhere, so I let him go and climb back into bed, holding his shirt to my nose and falling back to sleep with his scent to help bring me sweet dreams.

Sweet dreams do indeed come, but I'm ripped from them when Molly lets out a warning bark, then another. A loud thump follows, but I'm still too sleepy to realize something isn't right.

Her yelp pierces through the silence in the house and for the second time tonight, I'm ripped into a conscious state. Soft steps creak the floorboards in the living room. My heart jumps into hyperdrive and a rushing roar in my ears makes it difficult to hear.

*Did Luke step on Molly?* I wonder and strain my ears, listening but hear nothing except maybe a faint panting noise.

"Luke?" I call out and sit up in bed, but I'm only met with silence. The silence isn't like that of a sleeping home, but the silence of fear. The hairs on the back of my neck raise as I hear another creak of the floorboard near the entrance to the hallway that leads to our room.

Climbing out of bed, I grab my phone then stand, staring at the door. Everything about this moment screams not right, but I open it anyway.

Maybe Sarah is sneaking out and stepped on Molly, but why would she not answer me when I called for Luke? She knows I wouldn't care if she was hooking up with Eric.

Stepping softly through the open door and peering out into the hallway, I see nothing but darkness.

"Luke?" I call at the same time Eric appears at my right and covers my mouth and the scream I'm about to unleash. Pushing me back into the room, the sound of a gunshot cracks through the house and wood ricochets off my door. I fall to the floor with a scream, and Eric dives to the ground outside our door, scooting away from the entrance of the hallway.

"Hide!" Eric roars and another shot fires through the house, this time shaking me from my stunned confusion. I push myself out of sight from the gunman in the hallway.

Eric crouches at the corner and takes a deep breath, then snaps his arm around the corner and fires his gun I didn't see him holding.

My brain is unable to process what is happening, and I watch in stunned horror until another bullet pierces through the wall just above Eric's head.

Eric glances at me and signals for me to move but where? If I move forward, the gunman will see me; if I move to the left, I am met with the wall. My only option is to move to my right, toward the closet, but the gunman will see me moving. Hoping the darkness is enough to cover me, I crawl to the right when another shot goes off, hitting the bed inches from where my head is. I can't stop the scream that claws from my throat and the tears that burn my eyes blind me as I cover my head with my hands and stay crouched there.

This is not how I pictured my life ending. My life doesn't flash before my eyes, regrets do. Missed opportunities flash before them. I should have hugged Emily and Matt tighter. I should have called them and told them I loved them before they went to bed. I should have told Luke I loved him. I wish I could tell him so he knows, so he doesn't have to wonder when I'm gone. I wish Eric and Sarah weren't here so they could have a future together. I hope they survive this.

My lungs fight for oxygen and my heart is trying to beat out of my rib cage. So many regrets. I don't want to leave with all these regrets. I want a chance to see my kids grow into adults. I want to see Luke again and tell him that I love him. I don't want these regrets. I want to live. I want to fight, not cower here, playing regrets over and over in my head until I am no more. I want to fight.

Risking a glance out the hallway, Eric cranks his arm around the corner and shoots twice. Now's my moment. The moment I fight to live and dive forward, out of the gunman's line of sight. I scramble toward the closet but locking myself in there or in the bathroom will only delay the inevitable.

Another shot goes off, and I hear a groan come from the hallway. It's too close to be the gunman.

*Eric! Oh God, he's hurt!*

Frantically, I search my room for anything I can use as a weapon. Footsteps coming down the hall echo like loud explosions. He's getting closer.

I chance another quick glance over my bed to see how much time I have left when Eric pops up from his crouch and swings around the corner, arms extend and shoots chest-level down the hallway. Three rapid shots.

I don't hear silence after that, only a steady, high-pitch ring, and stare dumbfounded at Eric, who is still standing in the hallway with his arms extended.

"You shot me!" a man cries over the ringing in my ears, and Eric takes a step forward almost out of my eyesight.

"Slide your gun to me!" he barks, his gun now aimed toward the ground. "Now!"

I hear the man groan. "I'm bleeding."

"I said slide it now or I'll shoot you again," Eric yells and takes another step forward. I can only see his back.

"Amber?" Sarah softly calls from the hallway, but I don't see her.

"I'm okay," I call out to her. Am I? My heart is racing and my whole body trembles. The ringing in my ears hasn't stopped either, and I think I may be in shock.

Having move farther down the hall, Eric is completely out of sight. Sarah comes to the bedroom door and looks around with her phone to her ear. It illuminates her face, and I can see she's frightened but stays calm as she speaks into the phone. How is she so calm?

"The intruder has been shot," Sarah says into the phone but doesn't dare look down the hall. "Eric, the police are on their way."

"I'm sliding his gun toward you, Sarah, but don't touch it," Eric calls and I finally stand up on wobbly legs. "The intruder is Arnold Toppler."

*Arnold Toppler.* I know that name. How do I know that name? It's in my head, but shock, fear, and coming close to death has addled my ability to think, so I disregard it.

"Amber?" Sarah looks at me, scanning me from head to toe. "Are you hurt?"

"No," I whisper and take a shaky step toward my sister. She rushes in still holding the phone to her ear and hugs me tightly. She's shaking but continues to talk to the dispatcher on the phone, giving them details.

"Why are you here?" Eric growls from down the hall and it snaps me somewhat out of my stupor.

"Please, man, I'm going to die," the gunman groans. "I need help."

"Start talking and you won't," Eric says, and I take another shaky step toward the door. I

want to see the man who tried to kill me. I need to
see him. I need answers.

"I was hired."

"Hired to do what?"

"To . . . to kill his ex. Fuck, I'm bleeding.
Come on!" the man yells, the desperation in his
voice tugs at the nurse in me. I want to run in and
start putting pressure on his wounds, but I hold
back. This man's words glue me to the floor. *He
was hired to kill me. Who would hire someone to kill me?*

"Why?" Eric asks, wanting answers, too.

"Her ex wanted her gone, something about
life insurance," he moans.

Henry wanted me killed. If I hadn't heard
it from the man possibly dying in my hallway, I
wouldn't have believed it. Why have me killed?
None of this makes sense, and maybe the shock
I'm in makes it difficult to believe, but this has to
be some sort of mistake. Henry wouldn't do such a
thing.

Still shaken and dazed, I walk out of my
room and around the corner but stop there. I
don't want to get too close to the man who tried
to kill me, but I need to know what the heck is
going on.

"Why does Henry want me dead?" My
voice is hollow and detached, even a little shaky.

At some point, Eric turned on the hallway light and the man peers up at me with beady dark eyes filled with tears. There isn't any hate in those eyes, just an emptiness touched with fear over his own life.

"Please, you gotta help me. I'm dying. It hurts!" he whines, those eyes pleading with me and I feel a little queasy. Queasy over his request to help him when his job was to kill me. Queasy over hearing Henry wanted me dead.

"Why?" I choke out, fisting my hands and swallowing the bile that wants to claw up my throat. Sarah comes to my side, resting her hand on my shoulder.

"I don't know! I'm dying, come on. You have to help me. Aren't you a nurse?" he cries, big tears sliding down his face. He opens his mouth in a silent scream, drool dripping down his cheek as he turns onto his side.

"You said life insurance. What life insurance?" Eric uses his foot to roll the man onto his back. "You want the ambulance to come? Then you tell us everything, or you bleed to death on this floor."

I shoot Eric a glance before realizing he's bluffing. Sarah is still holding the phone to her ear.

An ambulance would have already been dispatched the moment she told them an intruder was shot.

"He had a life insurance policy on her, said if I made it look like a suicide, he would pay me double. Oh fuck, man, I'm getting dizzy."

Eric nudges the man with his foot. "Keep talking."

"I knew . . ." he trails off, inhaling short, quick breaths, which are starting to sound shallow. "I couldn't make it look like a suicide . . .. So, I was going to make it look like an accident . . .. But Henry wanted me to pin it on Luke."

*Pin it on Luke?*

"How?" I ask before Eric can.

"I broke into his shop," he says, his voice distant and his eyes roll around. "Found a gun he . . . keeps . . . in his office."

"What were you going to do with the gun?" Eric asks, getting down on one knee, still pointing the gun at Arnold and placing two fingers on his neck.

"I'm sorry," Arnold whispers. "I was going to shoot you and leave the gun."

He passes out.

# 23

## - Luke -

The shop is a mess of tools and materials thrown around the place. Two of my toolboxes have been knocked down, their drawers open and tools spilling from them. The tiny house I've been working on is untouched. Nothing appears to have been taken. A few tools may be broken, but mostly, it looks like whoever did this wasn't putting much effort into the crime they were committing.

"Only the one window was busted," I note to Sheriff McKnight, whose scratching his head and looking around. "Does this not seem odd to you?"

"I can't say I've never seen something like this but doesn't happen often. Probably teenagers who chickened out at the last second."

"Yeah, probably . . ." I mumble but don't really believe it.

"You sure nothing isn't missing, no cash or tools? Did you have any guns onsite?" McKnight asks.

"I didn't have any cash onsite and my tools look like they are all here, at least all the expensive ones. I have a gun I keep in my desk."

"Is it missing?" McKnight asks, glancing to where my office is in the back of the shop.

"I don't know, I didn't check," I say and head for my office. I didn't even think about the gun; I was more worried about the tools being stolen. "I didn't think to check."

"Why do you keep a gun at the shop?" McKnight asks casually, and I choose not to read into the question.

"I keep the few guns I own in Clint's gun safe at his place, but I kept this one at the house. I moved it to the shop when the kids and Amber moved in. Wasn't sure how she would feel about having a gun in the house." He nods, seeming to accept the answer, but if I have learned anything, it is that you can never trust a McKnight.

We walk into my office and the few papers, order forms, and receipts on my desk have been swiped off onto the floor. The table my coffee pot sits on had been shoved hard, leaving the items strewn across the table or on the floor. Walking around the desk, all the drawers have been yanked out, including the drawer that I stored my gun case—and it's completely empty.

"The gun's gone," I tell McKnight, not understanding why someone would steal a gun. Sure, it's worth a few hundred dollars, but I have tools worth three times that out on the shop floor.

"The gun was registered to you?" McKnight questions, eyeing the plans that are still tacked up in my office unharmed.

"Yeah, I have the paperwork on it somewhere in here," I mumble as I look around at the paper on the floor.

"Don't touch anything for now," McKnight says, then points at the plans. "Who is this for?"

"Clint is building a house for Dawn," I share, though I probably shouldn't. If McKnight tells his father about the build, he may become a thorn in my side. He retired as sheriff several years ago but is still heavily involved in the community. I'm following every code regulation and getting the permits required to build Clint's house, but I wouldn't put it past McKnight Senior to put up roadblocks if he gets wind of the project.

"Looks like a nice home. Lots of bedrooms."

"They want a lot of kids," I grunt. "Do you think this could be related to Amber's tire being slashed?"

"It's possible, but if you think Arnold Toppler has anything to do with this, know he lives in Kansas City and I've checked in with his employer. He's been showing up at work on time as scheduled," McKnight shares but something seems to be bothering him. His stoic expression reveals nothing, but something in the way he's looking around doesn't sit right.

"What are you not saying?"

"Amber's tire, now this . . . .. This isn't a coincidence. What are *you* not telling me?" McKnight fires back and my hackles raise.

"Sarah didn't fill you in on Amber's ex?"

"She said he's been causing some problems for Amber, asked me to put more patrols on your house, but that's all she shared," McKnight says.

"She didn't tell you that he threatened to make things difficult for Amber if I didn't end things with her?" I raise a brow, unsure how I feel about the underlying interrogation McKnight is throwing my way. Surely, he doesn't think I'm behind the tire slashing.

"Yeah, she showed me the video." McKnight nods then looks out where two of his deputies are standing by the broken window, nailing plywood over the now-empty space. "Something like this could cast some suspicion on Henry."

Waiting for further explanation, I slit my eyes at McKnight.

"Nothing was stolen, except for a gun. You've got evidence of Henry making a threat." McKnight watches me closely.

"What are you trying to imply?" I growl and clench my fists. Does he honestly think I would fake a burglary to pin on Henry?

"Henry doesn't seem like the petty crime type."

"McKnight," a deputy interrupts, waving him over and McKnight leaves the office.

I dig into my pocket for my phone. If McKnight thinks I'm trying to set Henry up, then I want to give Eric a heads-up so he can get in front of this. Searching my coat pockets, I can't find my phone. I must have left it in my truck, and I leave the office to get it.

McKnight holds his hand up, stopping me in my tracks. "Stay here for a moment, and don't touch anything."

I can't hear what the deputy is saying to McKnight, but his body stiffens as he finishes listening. Their conversation is making me uneasy. When McKnight finally responds to the deputy, the deputy side-eyes me before nodding and both turn to face me.

"Luke," McKnight says calmly, too calmly. My stomach drops. "I need to escort you to the station. There has been an incident."

# 24

## - Amber -

"Pick up, c'mon, pick up," I whisper into the phone. Luke hasn't answered any of my calls and none of my texts. It's been over an hour since the ambulance loaded Arnold and rushed him to the hospital. Eric was then loaded up into another ambulance for a bullet wound that had grazed his shoulder, and Sarah went with him after instructing me not to call Henry to check on the kids.

I'm going out of my mind with worry for them. Has Henry hurt them? Does he plan to hurt them? So many unsettling thoughts race through my head. All I want to do is make sure they are okay, but Sarah said one call to Henry could put them more in danger and I'm not willing to sacrifice my need to know they are okay over their well-being.

"I'm sure he's fine. He probably isn't checking his phone," my mom tries to reassure me as I pace across the kitchen floor.

A police officer is standing by the front door making sure nothing is touched and the crime scene stays preserved until a detective can come on-site—not that there is much to preserve. The front door was pried open and doesn't close fully, the crowbar used remains close by, and several bullet holes throughout the house surprisingly didn't leave much wreckage, just chunks of sheetrock and splintered wood.

I hadn't had time to really decorate the place fully, focusing on getting the necessities like a TV, couch, and bench in the mudroom. The only real decorating I had done was Christmas-related. Just this week we got a Christmas tree and used some of Luke's old childhood ornaments. The kids picked out new stockings but none of it was harmed.

My mother's phone goes off, and I stop my pacing to watch her answer, hoping and praying it's Luke, even though I know he would call me before he would call my mom. What can I say, desperation is a funny thing.

"Oh good, that's good news." She nods into the phone and for a moment, my heart thumps in relief that maybe it is Luke and he's okay. "I'll let her know. Okay. You're heading over there now?"

*It isn't Luke.*

*Where is he? Why hasn't he called? Did Arnold kill him before coming to kill me?* All these questions play on repeat in my head. A person can go mad with worry. Every time I try to reassure myself that Luke is okay, I am consumed with regret. Regret over not telling Luke that I love him. If he died without knowing, I think my world might crumble. The shoe finally dropped, and I may have missed my opportunity.

Getting myself worked up over the unknown isn't good for me. I know this, but my body won't stop moving and my mind keeps racing. I need to lay down, elevate my feet, and take calming breathes. I'm an ER nurse, I know what shock looks like and the effects it can have on a person, but all I want to do is get in my car and drive to Luke's shop and make sure he's okay. Unfortunately, the deputy standing by the door won't let me leave.

I pace back and forth, jumping from one worried thought to another. When I try to stop thinking about all my worries, I move to reliving the shooting. It's so surreal to learn someone wants you dead. No, not someone . . . my ex-husband.

It was no secret he had a want for money. I knew he wanted to be secure financially when we started dating—it's the kind of thing you talked about when you planned a future with someone. That want for financial security motivated him to build his insurance business. I never saw that as a bad quality. I shouldn't have overlooked how disconnected he became when he found out I was pregnant with Matt. I thought he was worried it would set him back on his goals, but somewhere down the line his wants shifted from financial security to wealth, and he put that want for wealth before me and the kids.

I thought when Henry married DeeDee his want for wealth wouldn't consume him so much and he would pay more attention to Emily and Matt. DeeDee was rich. Her trust fund alone was worth more than I would ever see in a lifetime, maybe even two lifetimes, but that didn't satisfy Henry. He continued to grow his insurance empire, barely paying any attention to his kids.

I didn't care that Henry was neglecting Emily and Matt because I knew together, the three of us were happy. We were content, and I couldn't force a relationship between Henry and his kids so I stopped paying attention to what Henry was doing, how his life might be going. He wasn't my concern anymore.

Now I can't help but wonder if I should have been paying attention. Would I have seen the signs that led him here? I know none of this is my fault, but will Emily and Matt see it that way? They are going to lose their father over this. How do I even begin to explain that?

"That was your father," my mom says, pulling me from my racing thoughts. "Molly is okay, but the vet wants to keep her for a few days for observation. She needed a few stitches, the crowbar cut her open pretty deeply, but she should be fine."

"Oh good." I sag in relief. When the police arrived, Eric relinquished his gun and let the police and paramedics handle Arnold while he rushed to Molly, who was panting in a pool of her own blood.

Arnold used the crowbar to pry open the front door and when Molly lunged for him, he hit her hard in the head and then again in the gut, tearing her open.

Eric would have taken her to the vet himself if the paramedics hadn't offered assistance. They stopped the bleeding and bandaged her up so my dad could take her to the vet. Only then did Eric allow the paramedics to look him over.

After the ambulance and police arrived, there was a whirlwind of activity that mostly blurred together. The paramedics checked everyone over, including me, but I couldn't leave, not until Luke returned. But now I wonder if I should have gone to the hospital. If Luke was rushed to the hospital, I could be with him now. We could be figuring out how we can get the kids away from Henry unharmed.

"Amber, I really think you should lay down," my mother pleads, stepping in front of me and blocking my path. She lays her hands on my shoulders before she pulls me in and hugs me. "Please lay down, you're going to make yourself sick with worry."

"Amber Baker?" a gentleman asks, coming through the front door. He's wearing jeans and his button-up shirt is slightly wrinkled but the badge he wears on his belt loop eases my stress some.

"I'm Amber."

"I'm Detective Dennison with Peak Valley PD. Are you up for a few questions?" he asks and all I do is nod. I'm not up for questions. I want to know how my kids are and where Luke is, but delaying the questioning means being stuck in this house longer.

"Alright, let's start from the beginning." Detective Dennison has me run through everything, only jumping in when he had a question or when he thought I needed a moment to collect myself. By the end of it, my chest had grown so tight I have a hard time breathing. Reliving it all over again for Dennison to hear made it less like a horrible dream I wish I could wake up from and more of a reality I have to live through, possibly alone, because Luke still hasn't called back and I still don't know if my kids are okay.

"I think that's all I have for now. I'm going to take a look around," Dennison says with a patient smile.

I'm about to ask him if he could have someone check on the kids and help me find Luke when Sheriff McKnight walks in, followed by

Luke. All the anxiety, fear, and stress washes a little bit away when he rushes over to me and pulls me into his chest.

He whispers something into my hair, and I think I tell him I love him over and over again. I don't know what he says to me; I'm too caught up in his embrace, feeling his chest rise and fall against my cheek. He is here, safe and unharmed. I squeeze tighter; I don't want him to disappear. Tears prick at my eyes until they begin to flow steadily down my cheek and soaks his shirt, but I don't think he cares. He just keeps holding me, his heartbeat steady in my ear, calming me with every thump. My breathing slows and syncs with his, and he keeps holding me.

"I'm sorry it took me so long to get back here," Luke whispers in my ear.

"Where were you? I thought you'd be back hours ago."

"That's my fault." McKnight steps closer to us. "I had Luke detained."

"Detained? Why?"

"It was precautionary. Once I heard what happened, I had him released and brought back here."

Hours could be passing us by, my mind still a maze of crazy thoughts and emotions, and

I'm tired, so tired, I just want to sleep. A deep dreamless sleep with Luke holding me together, but I still don't know anything about the kids.

"McKnight needs to talk with you, are you up for it?" Luke asks softly, tilting my head and scanning over every inch of my face. He releases me from his embrace and wipes my tears though it's useless as they just keep coming.

"Can you check on my kids first?" I choke out, turning to face McKnight, who has been patiently waiting with Detective Dennison.

"I'll see what I can find out," McKnight says, then points to a deputy. "Can you look into that?"

The deputy nods and grabs his radio on his shoulder and starts to speak into it while turning to leave.

"I'm not going to make you run through what happened again. We were able to question Arnold before he went into surgery," McKnight says, then points to the stool. I don't want to sit down; I want to know if my kids are safe and unharmed. "I need you to sit down."

Luke gently guides me to the stool and I sit, noticing for the first time that Sarah and Eric are also here.

"Your ex-husband is expecting to hear from Arnold letting him know that he finished the job, so we don't have a lot of time," McKnight says, waving for another person I didn't realize was there to come over.

"Don't have a lot of time for what? To arrest him?" I ask. A man walks over with a camera and a tackle box.

"To send him proof Arnold finished the job," Detective Dennison answers instead.

"I don't understand?"

"Amber, in order for Henry to be convicted and to make sure the charges stick, they are going to need more proof than just our testimony," Sarah explains gently but it feels more like a punch to the gut.

"Wh-what kind of proof?" I ask, my voice shaky and Luke tightens his grip on my shoulder.

Glancing up at Luke and seeing the way his jaw clenches, I know he already knows what they are going to ask me to do. Looking around at Eric then back to Sarah, I can tell they all do. What am I missing?

"They need Henry to think you're dead."

# 25

## - Luke -

I don't trust McKnight. I don't trust any of the
McKnights. Eric is right, the whole family is
rotten. I was willing to give him the benefit of the
doubt after helping Amber, but not anymore.

Fucking McKnight had me detained
because he thought I was trying to setup Henry.
Only I wasn't really detained, he made me go
through the routine of being arrested, treating me
like a fucking criminal.

I called Eric only to discover he was at the
hospital and that Arnold fucking Toppler broke

into my home and tried to kill Amber. I was sitting in a jail cell while McKnight went and figured out what happened, giving me no details. Luckily, Sarah was with Eric and demanded McKnight release me.

Only McKnight didn't send word to his deputies to release me. He waited until after he finished questioning Arnold and learned he was behind the break-in and was the anonymous caller to the police knowing they would have me come down, leaving Amber defenseless, did McKnight return to the station and bring me back to the house.

The asshole didn't even apologize, just shrugged and claimed he was doing his job. Couldn't rule anyone out. It's such bullshit.

I think he lost any chance he had with Sarah, which was slim before. She refused to speak to him. Eric now sees McKnight's actions as an act of war against the Colsons. Only we have to play nice with him while he helps lead the investigation on Henry.

I think we may need a new sheriff in Peak Valley.

I have endured a lot in my life, and I'll endure McKnight's fake hero act, but I'm barely holding it together and watching Amber get made up to look dead is almost my breaking point.

They have her posing in our bed, in my shirt that I put on her before being lured away, spraying a mist of fake blood around her.

Amber is trying to stay calm, trying to lay as if she is in a relaxed sleep but her body is stiff, she's tense, and the tears gut me every time one slides down her face.

"It's almost over, Amber, just try to relax," I say from the hallway where the bastard shot at her. *Where I should have been protecting her.*

"He has my babies," she whimpers from the bed, and I almost stop the tech from pouring fake blood on to the bed so I can hold her.

Knowing Henry has the kids, waiting for a response from the man he hired to kill Amber, rolls through my head on repeat. It doesn't feel right not saving them from the asshole's clutches. If the greedy bastard was willing to have Amber killed, then how do we know he won't hurt Emily and Matt?

"Can we speed this up?" I growl at the tech, who only pauses for a moment to glance at me before he looks over at Detective Dennison.

"Why don't you come with me?"
Dennison suggests, and I shake my head. I'm not
going anywhere.

"I have some questions for you," he says
and then has the nerve to look at Eric.

I glare at the detective. "I'm not letting
Amber out of my sight."

"Luke, there are details we need to run by
you about how this operation is going to work.
Amber is safe, Sarah will stay here and make sure
nothing happens while we go in the kitchen."

I'm about to protest but Eric steps in front
of me. His arm in a sling but his other grabs my
shoulder and tries to turn me away from Amber.

"You don't need to see this," Eric
murmurs, the seriousness gone and nothing but
concern washes over his face. "You don't want
this image in your head. It will haunt you for the
rest of your life."

Knowing he's right and wanting to argue
wages war in my head, but I let him turn me and
we walk away from a scene that *will* haunt me for
the rest of my life. Knowing I almost lost Amber
isn't something I'll ever forget.

"I'm going to run through the plan with
you. It's important that you know how the
operation will play out and what is expected, but

what's most important is that you cooperate and follow every instruction we give you." Dennison gets down to business once we are in the kitchen, too far away for Amber to hear.

"Understood," I mutter, running my hand down my face.

"I've been in contact with the Kansas City PD. They have an undercover officer who we think can be a decoy and can get the evidence we need to convict Henry."

"Decoy? What, to play Arnold? Henry will see right through that." I glare at Dennison, measuring the man for his worth. After McKnight's little stunt, my faith in Peak Valley PD has been shattered. So far, I haven't heard anything that makes me think they have this situation under control.

"Arnold only met with Henry once, and it was a month ago," Eric says, reading my frustration. "He's expected to send a text to Henry that the job is finished. Dennison did that from the phone found on Arnold. At two p.m. today, Arnold told McKnight he was supposed to meet with Henry at *Dave & Busters,* where he will get the rest of the money owed to him. It's a public place and will be easy for the decoy to play down his features."

"*Dave & Busters*? Henry plans to meet with the decoy while he has Matt and Emily?"

Dennison nods. "Yes, we believe so."

"Are we sure the kids are okay?" I ask again. I've asked all night, but no one has been able to give me a definitive answer.

"As far as we know, they are fine."

"How do we know he doesn't want to hurt them, too? He could have insurance policies on them also."

"We believe he will use them as alibis and play the doting father to deflect suspicion," Dennison reassures, but it does nothing to reassure me. When I don't say anything, he continues running through the plan. "The decoy will have a hidden police camera on him and show Henry the pictures of Amber and tell him how he set you up to take the fall. Once Henry hands over the money to the decoy, we will have officers step in to make the arrest."

"You'll just have this whole exchange go down in front of Matt and Emily?"

"The decoy has been instructed to make sure the children are not around while they make the exchange."

"It doesn't sound like it will work, but what choice do we have?"

"None. This plan will work, and it will ensure Henry gets convicted."

"I want to be there," I say, looking at Dennison. Nothing is going to stop me from watching Henry get what he deserves. "I have to be there."

"Both you and Amber will need to come up to Kansas City and be ready to take the kids once Henry is arrested, but you can't be on location until after the arrest is made."

"Not good enough," I snarl, stepping in close. "After the shit McKnight put me through, you owe me this."

Dennison nods. "I'll see what I can do."

"When do we leave?"

"We have some time. I suggest you pack some clothes, and I'll have one of the deputies take you somewhere for a few hours to sleep before we transport you to Kansas City."

"How am I supposed to sleep when Amber's ex tried to have her killed and has her kids?"

"I don't expect you to, but you should *try*. Tomorrow isn't going to get any better . . . not until this is over," Dennison says truthfully.

"Thank you," I say on an exhale.

"Don't thank me yet," Dennison says. "Thank me when this is over."

*****

"Amber?" I say softly from the door into the bathroom. I don't want to scare her, but everything scares her. She's jumpy and in shock, and I don't know how to help her, but I will do whatever it takes to make her feel safe again.

"I'm fine, Luke," she says when I shut the door so she can have more privacy. She pulls off my shirt, now covered in fake blood, and stares down at it as tears well up in her eyes. "I didn't tell you . . .. I should have told you sooner."

"Tell me what?"

"I love you. I should have told you sooner. I'm sorry I didn't tell you. I should have told you," she rambles, big tears rolling down her face as she looks up at me.

"Shh, it's okay. I love you, too." I pull her in my arms and she lets out a gut-wrenching sob that tears me up. She's never going to be the same after this, but I'll do everything in my power to restore her. To give her a sense of security and

chase away her fears. Knowing she loves me
makes this shitshow a little easier to wade through.

Amber's body shakes in my arms and I feel
it all. I let her cry until she has no more tears left,
then I take our clothes off and guide her into the
shower, washing away the fake blood, her tears,
and God, how I wish I could wash away her fears.

# Fight Forever

# 26

## - Amber -

I can't believe I'm watching this. The man who fathered my children, who used to be my husband, is laughing with Emily and Matt while they play whack-a-mole at *Dave & Busters*. I don't know why I expected him to be cold or distant, but definitely not happy. Not walking around like he doesn't have a care in the world, but here he is. He's *happy* about my death.

"Officer Crater is going in," the police officer says in front of the monitors displaying the different hidden camera feeds from all the undercover officers already scattered around the place.

Two displays have a view of Matt and Emily, and I have never felt so helpless just watching them play. I should be protecting Matt and Emily, shielding them from the horror that is about to unravel their lives, but I can't. I can't do anything but watch.

I didn't meet the man posing as Arnold, but I watch from his hidden camera as he approaches Henry. I look over at Luke, who is watching just as attentively as I am with his jaw clenched tight. Sensing my eyes on him, he looks at me before he leans over and grabs my hand and squeezes it. I don't think I would be able to get through this without him.

Henry looks up as if staring at me from the display and I feel nauseous when he squints then smiles at Officer Crater.

"Meet me at the bar," Henry says to him when he's a few feet away, then turns his back. I can't see what Henry does next and I frantically scan the displays for a better view. One monitor shows Henry say something to Matt before he leaves them at the whack-a-mole game.

Henry takes his time walking over to where Officer Crater is now sitting at the bar. A smug, almost gleeful smile spreads across his face as he orders two beers—one for himself and the other for his buddy.

"You don't have to watch this," Luke whispers next to me and his hand slides tenderly down the back of my hair. I relax a little, but the ill feeling in my stomach hasn't gone away.

"How did it go?" Henry asks Officer Crater after their beers arrive.

"It's done," Officer Crater grunts, then quickly takes a sip of his beer. The officer is good at downplaying his features. A hat is pulled down low over his forehead and he's wearing an oversized coat.

"Do you have proof?"

Officer Crater pulls a phone from his pocket and taps on it, pulling up the picture created last night and slides the phone over to Henry. He picks it up and stares at it for several seconds and when I think he's about to hand it back, he zooms in on the picture. Bile claws up my throat, but I swallow hard. I refuse to be sick. I have to watch this; I have to watch Henry prove he really did try to have me killed.

"You shot her?" Henry asks, looking closely at where the tech placed a fake bullet wound on my neck.

"Yeah, with the boyfriend's gun," Officer Crater shares, taking the phone from Henry's hand and pocketing it.

"And you made it look like he was the killer?" Henry narrows his eyes at Officer Crater, and I suck in a breath, afraid Henry has caught on.

"I left the gun for the cops to find," he says, and then Henry slaps his back like he's congratulating him.

Luke swears under his breath next to me and I squeeze his hand. He's just as disturbed by this as I am, but he's holding it together a lot better than I am.

Knowing it's almost over, I glance at the monitors that are recording Matt and Emily. They look happy playing games, and I wonder if they will be able to be happy after this.

"Here's what I owe you," Henry says, pulling an envelope from his inside jacket pocket and hands it to Office Crater. "If this blows back on me, the insurance fraud evidence I have on you will go to the police. I'll take you down right along with me."

"Understood," Officer Crater says, taking the money and gets up. That's when *Dave & Buster's* erupts in chaos.

Three men descend on Henry, but I don't watch his arrest. I don't hear the words he yells at Officer Crater, who is also being arrested. I search the monitors for Emily and Matt.

Two men move in on them, pulling their badges out for them to see, but Matt eyes them cautiously as they approach. Emily looks up at her brother while dropping the whack-a-mole hammer.

"Matt, Emily, you need to come with us," one of the officers says to them, both still holding their badges up.

"I want to find my dad," Matt says to them, then looks around the whack-a-mole game toward the bar. His eyes go wide when he sees the men kneeling over a cursing Henry.

"Your mom is outside waiting for you," the officer says. Emily clutches her brother's arms and my vision floods with tears. I want out of this vehicle. They look so small on the monitor, so innocent. They don't deserve this. None of this.

"Can we go and get them?" Luke asks, ready to leave the utility van they told us we had to wait in. Luke wouldn't let them keep us at the station and demanded we be on location. They only allowed it when Detective Dennison vouched for us, promising he would make sure we stayed put in the utility van until he gave us the green light to leave.

"As soon as they take Henry to the station," Dennison says, watching the monitors at my side.

"What do I tell Matt and Emily?" I say to Luke, realizing I have no idea how to explain this to them.

"Little as possible for now," he says, pulling me to his side and kissing my temple.

"We don't want Henry to know you are still alive. Not until we have questioned him." Dennison watches the vehicle Henry is being loaded in. Long, torturous minutes tick by before the cruiser holding Henry locked in the back drives off in the opposite direction from us.

Dennison finally opens the utility van door but doesn't let us exit. The two officers who approached Matt and Emily exit *Dave & Buster's* and head toward us. I look at Dennison, who steps aside, and I'm running the moment my feet hit the ground. My only thoughts are to grab them, hug them, and shield them from everything.

"Mommy!" Emily calls out, holding her arms wide so I can scoop her up. I pull her into me and hug her tight, unable to stop the tears that spill out. I won't ever let them go

I pull Matt into my hug, squeezing him. He doesn't protest but says something to Luke. I have no idea what was said, I just want to hug them, smell them, breathe in their sweet scent, and just be thankful they are safe in my arms.

Fight Forever

# 27

## - Luke -

"Tell Jax thank you for me. You can't even tell this place was shot up," Amber says, snuggling into my side. We made it home earlier this evening after we finished meeting with the Kansas City detectives and social services. While we were gone, Benny and Jax got to work on the house, fixing the drywall, replacing our bed with a new mattress, and even replacing our door. Benny didn't want Amber to be reminded of the horrific events she has had to live through. For that, I will be forever thankful.

Social workers were available when we took the kids to the Kansas City police station. They helped us break the news as best we could to Emily and Matt that they won't be seeing their father any time soon.

"Why?" Emily had asked, swinging her feet in the chair. Both the kids were given some snacks to munch on and she eagerly ate hers.

"You father has to go away for a very long time, and I'm not sure when you will be able to talk to him," Amber said, looking at the social worker for reassurance. She nodded and gave Amber a sympathetic smile.

"Is he in jail?" Matt asked, visibly upset.

"He is in jail, yes."

"What did he do?" Emily frowned, realizing her father wasn't going away on a trip, but going away where she knew bad men went.

"He did something very bad."

"Oh . . .." She looked to Matt, who nodded.

After that, there was little talk about Henry. The social workers gave Amber some contacts for counseling and encouraged her to set up an appointment for the kids after the holidays. I think it would be good for them all. Help them get adjusted to their new life without their father.

Charges were made and Henry was arrested, but until he goes before a judge, we won't know what will happen next.

Now we are home, sitting in a new limbo. There is so much I want to talk to Amber about, yet I don't want to worry or overwhelm her.

"It was nice of Jax to have pizza delivered," Amber says, pulling me from my thoughts.

"Underneath all that wild, he's a pretty nice guy."

"Yeah."

"Are you getting tired?" I ask her, though it's only nine and the kids went to bed not that long ago.

"I want to stay here and listen for the kids," she says quietly. "Is that weird?"

"No."

"I know they are safe. We are safe, but I'm just . . .."

"Worried?" I ask, tucking her hair behind her ear. My hand caresses down her neck and arm.

"Yeah." She sighs. "Do you think they will be okay?"

"The kids? Yes."

"You're so confident about that."

Amber lifts her head to search my face.

291

"It has always been you who gave them a home; you made them feel safe and loved. I don't think they got that from Henry. Their routine isn't going to change. They have friends and family who love them and will support them. Yes, what Henry did was devastating, but it won't break them. I'm more worried about you."

"I'm fine," she says and lays her head down again, but I lift it up to see her face.

"Are you fine?"

"Of course."

"If this place . . . doesn't feel safe for you anymore, we can move. I want you to feel safe."

"What that man did entering our home and . . .." She doesn't finish her sentence. Instead, she looks away and sucks a breath. "I can't let him win."

"Let him win?"

"Henry," Amber says, sitting up and faces me. "Henry tried to take so much from me. If I let what he tried to do scare me out of this house—a house I have started to dream of a future in—I feel like Henry wins. If I let what he tried to do scare me, he will still have power over me. Power I don't want him to have. I refuse to be scared over what happened. But mostly, I refuse to let him take the one thing that has become so important to me these last few weeks."

"What?" I ask when she doesn't immediately answer.

"The family you and I are starting to build here in this home. I don't want Henry to have that win."

"I love you." I pull her into my lap and kiss her gently at first before running the tip of my tongue across her bottom lip. Amber shifts in my lap, straddling him, and my dick goes rock-hard.

"I love you, Luke," she whispers against my mouth then bites my lip. I pull her closer, needing to feel close to her, then tuck my hands under her ass and stand. She wraps her arms tightly around my neck and holds on.

"I'm going to marry you," I say against her ear and she stiffens in my arms.

She leans back to look at me, not saying anything at first, simply staring at me before she smiles. "Okay."

"Okay."

"Yeah, okay."

"Okay, then." I chuckle, then walk her around the couch and down the hallway to our room. Dropping her unceremoniously, I crawl in after her. She laughs, scooting backward, stopping when her back hits the headboard and I keep crawling until I hover over her.

I like the way she gazes at me. For the first time in the last twenty-four hours, she doesn't look worried or distressed.

Caging her against the mattress, both my hands beside her shoulders, I peer down, craving her more than I ever have before. There is no going back now. Not ever. She's mine and will be mine for the rest of our lives as soon as I can make that happen.

"Why are you looking at me like that?" Amber's smile falters.

"You're mine," I whisper, leaning down so I can kiss her shoulder, sliding my nose along her collarbone and nuzzle her neck.

Amber tugs on my shirt, pulling it up until I have to break free from her neck to pull it over my head. She sits up and removes her shirt, and I watch in awe as she takes off her bra, letting her breasts fall free and my mouth waters.

"Take my pants off," I order, and she obliges while I unbutton her jeans and slide a hand inside, too impatient for her to take them off. My fingers grab ahold of her pussy and she hums in response. "You're soaked."

"I want you," she whispers, her eyes black with desire. I have never wanted her more.

Tugging her pants and panties, she quickly helps me take them off. She's naked beneath me and it is the most beautiful sight I have ever laid eyes on.

I skim my fingers across her skin, between her breasts, down her soft stomach, detouring around her core over her hipbone and down her inner thigh. She shivers with anticipation and my dick throbs to be let loose. Standing from the bed, I watch her watch me remove my pants, leaving my boxer briefs. She licks her lips, waiting to see me take them off and for a moment, I want to tease her, but I need her and rip them off.

Climbing back onto the bed, I set my sights on her wet pussy and my mouth is on her, devouring her. Her taste and scent are intoxicating, igniting something deep in my chest. I torture her in the most delicious way, licking and sucking. Her hands tug at my hair as she breathlessly moans my name.

"I'm going to come," she pants as her hips arch up. I lick and swirl my tongue faster, slowly dipping one finger inside her, then another, and she tenses around them, pulling me in and coming hard. Such beautiful noises come from that mouth of hers.

Kissing my way back up her body, she lays sedated across the bed, her hair feathered out. I want to pound my chest knowing I did that and she's all mine. Grazing my lips across hers, she smiles and wraps her arms around my neck before pushing me onto my back.

"I want to be on top," she says, her fading orgasm still flushing her skin. She looks pink and soft and so fucking perfect. She takes ahold of me; I clench my jaw when she lines me up and slides my dick inside her. Grabbing her hips, I pull her down hard. Her breath catches and for a moment, we are both completely dazed by the feel of each other.

Her hands land on my chest and she slowly rocks against me. I let her take charge, sliding my hands up her sides before palming her breasts and she lets out a whimper when I pinch her hardened nipples. Leaning forward, I take one into my mouth, swirling my tongue. My other hand drops to her clit and matches her rhythm as she grinds faster against me.

I know she's close. I feel her swell and tense around my dick, and I want to come with her. Releasing her breast, I grab her hips and thrust, feeling her begin to pulse. Thrusting harder, we are both ready to let go.

"Oh God, I'm going to come," she whimpers.

"Let go, darlin'." I circle her clit until she does, thrusting hard once more inside her, and release. She falls onto my chest, both our hearts pounding as the buzz of our orgasm wipes the last of our energy.

"That was amazing."

"It's always amazing with you," I whisper into her ear.

"Mmm."

Pulling and tugging the comforter from under us, I'm finally able to cover us, not letting her move from where she lays on top of me.

"I love you," I say before sleep takes us both.

Fight Forever

# 28

## - Amber -

"Wake up, Jax," I sing to the man-child sleeping on my couch. "Time to wake up."

"No," he grumbles, but peels one eye open and then another, seeing the coffee I'm holding out for him. "For me?"

I nudge it toward him. "Yes, sir."

"Thanks."

"Mind telling me why you're sleeping on our couch?"

"Burns found out about the stripper and kicked me out when I told him Miss Janet had a great time," Jax says around a yawn, sitting up and taking the coffee.

"Why would you do a silly thing like that?" I laugh and pat his shoulder.

"He found out I stole his Polaroid. I was deflecting."

"Oh, because deflecting is always a good strategy." I roll my eyes and walk into the kitchen.

"Mom!" Matt yells down the stairs. "I can't find my tablet."

"It's in the living room," Luke answers for me, coming around the corner into the kitchen. "Morning." He smiles coyly at me.

"Morning." I return the smile and lean up against his chest, giving him a big kiss.

"Someone looks happy this morning," Sarah says, rounding the island and heads straight for the coffee. "Wouldn't be due to the ruckus I heard next door, would it?"

"What in Bob Barker is going on? Did all the Colsons and Bakers stay here last night?" I glare at her.

"Clint and Dawn are happily at home," Jax chimes in, taking a seat at the island.

"Hey, Jax." Matt fist bumps him and sits.

"Where is Emily? I'm going to be late for work if she doesn't hurry." I side-step Luke and yell, "Em, hurry up. We gotta go!"

"I thought I would take them to Mom and Dad's," Sarah says, leaning against the counter, blowing on her coffee.

"So you don't have to explain to your parents why didn't come home last night?" Eric asks, coming around the corner.

Sarah narrows her eyes at Eric. "Yes."

"Are you sure you want to take them?" I ask, but it would give me a chance to relax a little before going into work. Luke wanted me to take a few days off after the incident with Henry, but the social workers suggested we maintain a normal routine to help make things easy on the kids. Christmas is only a few days away and the kids are getting excited. They don't even seem fazed by the whole ordeal.

Henry is still maintaining his innocence and when he went before a judge, he pleaded not guilty, which means a trial will happen. Sarah warned us that we would likely have to testify against him. I'm not looking forward to that, but the trial hasn't been scheduled yet, so I have some time to prepare.

Arnold Toppler pleaded guilty and from what Sarah has been able to get from Sheriff McKnight, he took a plea deal in return for testifying against Henry.

For now, we maintain a routine, though it feels a little like living through limbo until we know what will happen with Henry.

"I'm ready! I brushed all my teeth. See?" Emily hooks her index finger in the corner of her mouth and opens wide.

"Missed a spot, squirt," Jax points out.

"Did not!" She slams her hands on her hips and sticks her tongue out.

"Come closer and I'll show you." Jax waves her over and when she steps closer with her mouth wide open, he scoops her up and tickles her. Loud squeals blare across the kitchen.

"I'm going to pee!"

"Okay, I guess you brushed all your teeth." Jax sets her down and taps her nose.

"Alright, kiddos, you ready to head to Grandma's?" Sarah asks, clapping her hands.

"Can I go with Luke and help at the shop?" Matt asks, looking hopeful at me.

"Fine with me, but I'll put you to work," Luke says smiling, but he glances at me to make sure I'm okay with it. I simply nod as my heart swells with more love than I knew I could have for a man. Not that long ago my life was falling apart. First, the fire that consumed my house, then Luke walking back into my life, and Henry trying to take everything, including my life, away from me. It all seems like a distant memory when I'm surrounded by family.

*How did I get so lucky?*

Fight Forever

# 29

## - Luke -

"Ho, ho, ho, Merry Christmas!" Burns bellows as he comes through the front door dressed in a Santa suit with a fake beard and all.

"Why is Santa skinny?" Emily asks, climbing onto my lap.

"Em, that's Burns." Matt rolls his eyes. He's sitting close to the Christmas tree eyeing the presents, waiting patiently for everyone to get here. It's early, the sun isn't even up, but everyone wanted to watch Emily and Matt open presents, even if it meant coming over at six a.m.

The Colson men haven't had a Christmas since our mom died. Over the last several months we have all managed to be in Peak Valley at the same time, too. Before this year, I can't remember the last time all four of us were together. I like having them around and hope they keep coming around.

"Santa Burns has presents!" Burns says in a jolly voice. Emily giggles when Burns pretends he can't carry the oversized red sack filled with presents.

"Quick scaring the children, old man," Benny calls from the couch, sipping some coffee.

"I'm not scaring the children. Am I scaring you, Emily?"

"No!" Emily laughs and Burns boops her nose.

"Sorry we are late. Burns insisted on dressing up," Miss Janet apologizes, patting my shoulder.

"He was also a bear to wake up," Jax says, taking the sack from Burns and carrying it over to the Christmas tree.

"What are you wearing, old man?" Eric asks as he comes down the hallway, Molly following close behind. Molly was released a few days after being hurt by the hitman and has been recovering well.

"Quit calling me an old man. I'm Santa Burns," Burns grumbles. "I'm getting some coffee."

"I'll join you," Miss Janet says with a wave.

"He's going to be grumpy," Clint grunts.

"He'll perk up when he gets some food in him." Jax yawns again, taking a seat next to Matt on the floor. "I plan to put myself in a food coma."

"Can we open presents now?" Emily asks, bouncing in my lap.

"Yes, go get your mom." Emily jumps off my lap and runs into the kitchen where the women have been brewing coffee and preparing breakfast.

The house has smelled like Christmas cookies for weeks now, and with each passing day since the incident with Henry and the hired hitman, everyone has begun to let the Christmas spirit take over.

Both the kids were confused at first, not understanding completely what their dad had done, but Amber and I both thought it best if they got a watered-down version of the truth. We will give them the full truth when they get older, but for now, our goal is to make them happy.

"You're going to love my present, Matt. I'll be your favorite uncle after this." Jax winks at Matt. That is another new development. Emily started referring to my brothers as her uncles and they have been eating it up, competing for the title of favorite uncle.

"Please, they both will call *me* their favorite uncle once they get my present," Eric scoffs, taking a seat next to Matt on the floor with a mug of coffee. Molly curls up by his feet.

"I see you boys are arguing for favorite uncle, but know I will always hold the favorite aunt title," Sarah says, pulling up a stool behind the couch.

"Until I make them their favorite brownies." Dawn laughs and moves to sit on Clint's lap.

"Alright, Emily and Matt, you both know the rule, one present at a time," Amber says, taking a seat next to me and handing me a mug of coffee.

"Thank you, darlin'." I throw my arm around her and pull her close.

Christmas erupts in a frenzy of wrapping paper, candy stealing from the kids, and Burns and Benny's bickering.

Emily and Matt were more than spoiled today. Each Colson brother tried to win that coveted favorite uncle slot.

We finally take the kids to the garage to show them their bikes. Emily squealed when Clint and Dawn gave her a unicorn helmet and glittery ribbons for the handlebars. Jax was pleased to see he put it together properly and tried to get her to pop a wheelie before Amber intervened.

Matt went nuts over his dirt bike and suited up in his gear. Jax and Clint ran through how to ride it and started it up, giving him pointers and throwing in some safety tips to ease Amber's anxiety. It's too cold for us to stay out for long, so we made our way back into the house, hungry for some biscuits and gravy.

"Mind telling Eric I'm your favorite uncle?" Jax asks Matt while we file into the kitchen from the mudroom.

"He hasn't received my final present yet." Eric smirks then winks at Matt.

"What do you mean . . . final present?" Jax narrows his eyes at Eric.

"You think after the dirt bike I was going to let you win so easily?"

"Remember who fixed that dirt bike up," Clint chimes in.

"Sneaky bastards," Jax mutters.

"I really hope you ran this past Amber," I whisper to Eric when he walks past me.

"Run what past me?" Amber asks, sneaking up behind me.

"Eric's gifts for the kids."

"Umm, yes? The riding gear and Emily's dollhouse, right?" Confused, she looks at Eric.

"Yeah, I may have forgotten to talk with her . . .." Eric rubs the back of his head. "In my defense, I thought you would have at least told her."

"No, I didn't tell her." I cringe, seeing Amber eye us both suspiciously. This may not end well. "Do not give them their presents yet." I point to Eric. "Not until Amber signs off."

"No, let's see what Eric got the kids," Jax speaks up by the island while he makes a plate of biscuits and gravy. "Right, Emily and Matt? You want your presents from Uncle Eric, don't you?"

Still wearing her unicorn bike helmet, Emily jumps up and down. "I want my present!"

"What's going on?" Burns asks, fixing himself four biscuits and gravy.

"Amber is about to kick Luke and Eric's ass." Sarah laughs, pouring orange juice in a pitcher half-full of champagne. "Amber, you are going to want a mimosa for this."

Eric frowns at Sarah. "Not helping."

Emily tugs on Eric's hand. "I want my present."

"Alright, cutie." Eric pats her head with an affectionate smile. "Get your brother and sit on the couch."

"Yay!" Emily hugs Eric. "Matt, come sit!"

"On a scale of one to ten, how mad am I going to be?" Amber asks, taking Sarah's mimosa.

"I'm hoping a one," I mutter, running a hand down my face.

"I'm betting a ten," Burns says, taking a seat at the dining table next to Jax.

"You know what Eric got them?" Amber asks.

"Nope, but it's Eric, and the look on Luke's face is priceless. Wish I had my camera." Burns glares at Jax, who chokes a little on his biscuits and gravy.

"I told you, old man, I can't remember where I put it," Jax mutters.

"*Liar.*"

"Burns, leave him alone. You got a nice digital camera from the boys," Miss Janet reprimands.

"I don't know how to use that stinking thing. It's got too many bells and whistles."

"Okay, kiddos, close your eyes," Eric calls from down the hallway, cutting off Burns' tantrum.

"They're closed," Matt says, then covers his sister's eyes with his hand.

Eric holds two squirming German Shepard puppies, and Amber gasps in horror then turns and mouths, '*You are in so much trouble.*'

"Oh, shit . . ." Jax mutters over a full mouth of food. "That isn't fair!"

Leaning against Clint's chest, Dawn sighs as she watches the kids. "They are so cute."

"Keep them eyes closed." Eric comes around the couch and places the puppies on their laps and Emily squeals.

Both the kids open their eyes wide and pick up the puppies in their laps. Emily immediately picks her puppy up and hugs it while Matt stares at his in shock, unsure if it is real.

"We each get one?" Matt whispers to Eric, who nods. Matt picks up the squirming pup and it licks his face, making him laugh. Molly isn't too interested in the puppies but is watchful from where she lays in her bed by the Christmas tree.

"You have to train them and take care of them so they grow up to be your best friend like Molly's mine."

"You've had them here this entire time?" Amber asks.

"Linda and Benny were holding on to them for me," Eric says, and Amber turns to look at her Mom and Dad, who only shrug.

"Really Mom? Dad?" Amber shakes her head but can't hide her smile.

"You should propose," Burns suggests, pointing at me with his fork full of food. "That'll get you out of the doghouse. Ha, get it?" He elbows Jax, who rolls his eyes.

"I already asked her," I blurt out, pulling Amber to my side.

"What?" everyone says at once, including Amber.

"When?" Sarah asks, her eyes wide.

"Yeah, I would like to know when this supposed proposal took place, too." Amber pushes me.

"A few days ago," I say, giving her a dumbfounded expression.

"No, you didn't." She slams her hands on her hips.

"Did he get on one knee, because that jackwagon didn't," Burns butts in, pointing at Clint.

"Shut it, Burns," I growl, looking around at everyone's shocked faces.

"No, answer him. Did you get on one knee?"

"No," I groan, running a hand down my face in frustration. "You seriously don't remember me telling you I was going to marry you?"

"You can't *tell her* you're going to marry her, you jackwagon!" Burns cries out, shaking his head. "You gots to *ask*!"

"That was your proposal?" Amber's eyes go wide, dropping her hands from her hips.

"Um . . . yes?" I cringe.

"What did she say?" Linda asks, taking a step closer, glancing between the two of us.

"She said okay."

"Is Mommy marrying Luke?" Emily tries to ask Eric quietly, but she doesn't have a low volume.

Eric laughs. "Sounds like it."

"Oh, good gravy, I did say yes." Amber covers her mouth, looking shocked.

"Get on one knee and ask again," Burns whisper-yells and this time, Miss Janet smacks him on the back of the head. "What? I'm trying to help the jackwagon."

Amber points at me. "Do not get on one knee!"

"Why not?" I frown. "Wait, let me get something."

I rush down the hall into our bedroom, hearing the murmurs as I go. Entering the closet, I pull the little velvet box I stashed away two days after Amber agreed to marry me. I had planned to give it to her over New Year's but now is as good of a time as any.

"Okay, so am I not supposed to get on one knee?" I ask, coming around the corner, holding the velvet box out for Amber to see.

"She said yes, put a ring on it!" Amber's mom cries out with tears in her eyes. Benny pulls her to his side.

Amber is looking at the box and I can't determine what the looks she has on her face means and my heart speeds up.

"You bought a ring?" Her voice sounds thick and tears brim the rim of her eyes.

"Of course." I chuckle, taking a step closer to her, opening the box for her to see the classic princess cut diamond engagement ring.

"Say yes, Mommy!" Emily and Matt stand a few feet away, clutching their puppies with smiles. I also meant to talk to them about the proposal, but thanks to Burns, I was ambushed. Granted, I should have kept my mouth shut, but I wanted everyone to know Amber's mine. That she will always be mine.

"Yes." Amber nods as a single tear slides down her cheek.

"Oh, thank God." Burns sighs. "I thought she was going to reject the jackwagon."

Ignoring Burns, I pull Amber into a tight hug and kiss her hard before pulling back and making sure my ring is on her finger so we can have our forever.

Amanda Lee Dixon

# Acknowledgements

Deepest love and appreciation to my family who has supported me while I venture down this amazing journey. I love you all so much.

Madelyn you have been a great sounding board, thank you. You are an amazing woman and I am so very proud of you.

To my husband thank you for your support and encouragement.

Rachael Leissner you came to me in my hour of need and have been a tremendous help! Thank you so much! I appreciate everything you have done and feel so lucky we were able to connect.

The Next Step PR, thank you for promoting my book and providing some much-needed guidance. You ladies are amazing, and I am so happy I was able to work with you all.

To my readers, thank you for taking the time to read and share my book. I am so grateful to each and every one of you!

# *About The Author*

Amanda Lee Dixon lives in the weather crazed Midwest with her husband, three teenagers and two mouthy malamutes. When she isn't working on the Peak Valley Forever Series, she is obsessively reading romance and fantasy books or pen shopping. Her weaknesses are colorful pens, planners and coffee.

Connect with Amanda now:
Website: www.amandaleedixon.com

www.ingramcontent.com/pod-product-compliance
Lightning Source LLC
Chambersburg PA
CBHW020250200626
46816CB00001BA/217